Disney

HIGH SCHOOL MUSICAL

STORIES FROM EAST HIGH #5

BROADWAY DREAMS

By N. B. Grace

Based on the Disney Channel Original Movie
High School Musical, written by Peter Barsocchini

Bath New York Singapore Hong Kong Cologne Delhi Melbourne

First published by Parragon in 2008
Parragon
Queen Street House
4 Queen Street
Bath BA1 1HE, UK

ISBN 978-1-4075-1743-8

Printed in UK

CHAPTER ONE

"**S**tudents! Settle down! Settle, please!" Ms Darbus, the drama teacher, tried to quieten the room. Everyone who was going on the big senior class trip – this year it was to New York City! – had gathered, and she could barely be heard over the din. Ms Darbus clapped her hands and yelled again, "I need quiet, please!"

But the noise continued – until Coach Bolton stepped to the front of the classroom, put two fingers in his mouth and let out an ear-piercing whistle.

1

Instantly, the room went silent. "That's better," he said. "Now, I know you are all excited about going to the Big Apple, but let me make one thing perfectly clear: Ms Darbus and I are your chaperones on this trip, which means we are responsible for your safety and well-being, which means that when one of us says to settle down, you had better settle! Understood?"

Everyone nodded meekly.

"Excellent. Ms Darbus, you have the floor."

"Oh, well . . . thank you, Coach Bolton," the drama teacher said.

She smiled graciously and stepped to the front of the classroom (or, as she preferred to think, centre stage). "Indeed, we are about to embark upon a grand journey together, an adventure that none of us will ever forget, a trip that will live on in our memories forever–"

Chad Danforth grinned at his buddy Troy Bolton, then pretended to snore.

"And that's not all! I have some very exciting news!" she continued, pointedly ignoring him.

After a long pause to make sure everyone's attention was where it should be – on her – she went on. "All of you have heard of *Last Bell!*, I hope?"

Most of the students looked puzzled, but Ryan Evans's hand shot into the air. "Yes, of course!" he cried out. "It's one of the most successful Broadway musicals of the last five years!"

"Oh, how could I have missed that?" Chad asked, rolling his eyes.

"It's set in a high school just like this one," Ryan went on. "I know all the songs by heart!" He got a faraway look in his eyes and added dreamily, "Sometimes I imagine what it would be like to appear on Broadway in a show like that. I could do it, I know I could–"

"And now you may have your chance," Ms Darbus said.

That caught the attention of Ryan's sister, Sharpay Evans. Her head whipped around. "What?"

Ms Darbus beamed at her. "Yes! The producers

have decided to hold open auditions for teenagers around the country! They'll choose a new cast that will perform the musical – on Broadway! – for one night only as a promotional event!"

Sharpay gasped. "This is it!" she said to Ryan. "Our destiny, our fate, our *future* has arrived!" She paused, then added, *"Finally."*

"Now, before you get too excited . . ." Ms Darbus held up a cautionary hand. "Hundreds of other high school students will also be auditioning. The competition will be fierce!" She relaxed enough to beam at Sharpay and Ryan. "Although I'm sure that East High students are among the most talented and well-prepared in the country!"

Sharpay beamed back, knowing that when Ms Darbus said 'East High students', she really meant her, Sharpay, the best actress that East High had seen in . . . well, forever.

Oh, and she meant Ryan, too, of course.

Sharpay's hand shot up into the air. "Ms

4

Darbus, what will the producers want us to do for our auditions? Should we prepare a monologue, or a dance routine, or a song, or maybe all three? And what about costumes? I know we're each allowed to bring just one suitcase on this trip, but surely those of us who are going to bring glory and renown to East High should be given an extra luggage allowance? Oh, and what about head shots and personal makeup cases and–"

"Somebody should call and warn the producers," Chad muttered to his buddies Troy, Zeke Baylor and Jason Cross. "They may want to start planning their escape route now."

Unfortunately, his voice wasn't quite low enough.

"Thorough preparation is the sign of a true professional!" Sharpay snapped at him. "Not that I would expect *you* to know anything about being a pro!"

"That's not true," Zeke said.

Chad grinned at him. "Thanks, buddy–"

"Chad is a pro at eating. He can finish off

five hamburgers in 15 minutes!" Zeke finished.

Chad shoved him, and Zeke started laughing. Ms Darbus just rolled her eyes. If only she were chaperoning serious, dedicated students like Sharpay and Ryan, instead of all these . . . *basketball* players!

Coach Bolton had had enough run-ins with Ms Darbus in the past to recognize the warning signs of a full-scale tantrum. "Okay, enough with the chatter," he said hastily. "Let's go over the rules of the road again. We're meeting tomorrow at the airport at six a.m. Everyone gets to bring one suitcase – *one*, Sharpay, I don't care how many costumes you have! – and everyone is going to have to report in twice a day while we're in New York. Also, Principal Matsui wanted me to remind you that–" he glanced down at a paper he was holding, " '–this trip is supposed to be educational, so you should focus on visiting sites of historical and cultural importance'. Is that absolutely clear?"

Everyone nodded solemnly, but their eyes were sparkling with excitement. They were going to New York City! With their best friends! What could be better?

The bell rang and they all burst into the hall, heading for their form rooms.

"This is going to be a blast," Troy said to Gabriella Montez. "What's the first thing you want to do in New York?"

"I have to go with Taylor to the television studio in the afternoon," Gabriella reminded him.

His face fell. "Oh. Right. The *College Quizmaster* show. I forgot."

"Man, I can't believe you guys actually made it to the finals!" Chad exclaimed.

"Well, we didn't have much competition," Taylor McKessie said complacently. "Even in that last round, Gabriella and I outscored the second place team by 50 points."

"You guys are awesome," Zeke said. "Serious brainiacs. Remind me to call you for tutoring when finals roll around."

Chad shook his head in mock sadness. "Too bad you'll have to study the whole time you're in New York, and Sharpay and Ryan are going to be rehearsing the whole time. Man, I'm glad that I won't have anything to do on this trip but enjoy myself!"

"Seriously," Jason agreed. He flipped open the guidebook that he'd been carrying everywhere for the last month. "What should we do first, the Statue of Liberty or the Metropolitan Museum of Art?"

Chad looked at him as if he'd grown an extra head. "Dude, there's no contest! The number one thing we gotta do is check out Madison Square Garden!"

The other boys nodded. They couldn't wait to see the arena where the New York Knicks played.

"What about Little Italy?" Zeke asked.

"Madison Square Garden," Chad said firmly. After a moment, he asked, "Why? What's in Little Italy?"

Zeke's smile lit up the hall. "I have two words

for you: awesome pastries."

"Okay, you have a point," Chad conceded. "But basketball comes first. Cookies come second."

"Cannoli," Zeke corrected him. "And don't forget tiramisu!"

"What about the Bronx Zoo? It's one of the best zoos in the world." Jason had his nose buried in his guidebook again. "When are we going to fit that in?"

"After Madison Square Garden," Chad replied. "First basketball, *then* bakeries, *then* the Bronx."

"Okay, but my book says that Central Park is a 'must-see'," Jason insisted. "So we must see that, too . . . "

As the three boys and Taylor walked down the hall to their next class, still arguing about their itinerary, Troy and Gabriella looked at each other and laughed.

"I think this is going to be the textbook definition of a 'whirlwind tour'," he said.

"Yeah," she agreed, looking wistful. "I just hope I get to do some fun stuff with you guys."

"You're only going to be on the quiz show for a few hours on Monday, right?" Troy asked. "That leaves plenty of time for, oh, I don't know. A stroll through Central Park? With, maybe, pretzels for two?"

Hanging out with Troy was always fun, but hanging out in New York . . .

Gabriella smiled at the thought, but then shook her head. "If we win the first round on Monday—"

"Which you will!" he said loyally.

"—then we'll have to go back to film again on Tuesday. And if we win on Tuesday—"

"Oh, right." Troy looked glum. "The finals are on Wednesday. And then we fly home the next day." He hesitated, then admitted, "I know this quiz show is a big deal and everything, but I wish we were going to have more time together."

"Taylor and I may not make it past the first round," Gabriella pointed out. "In which case we'll have plenty of time . . . "

"Hey, you can't think like that," Troy said. "You gotta think like a winner! You guys are unbeatable!"

"I hope so. The grand prize is a college scholarship for each person on the winning team," she said. "It would help my mum a lot if I could win that."

"You've got a great shot," he reassured her. "And don't worry. After all, New York is the city that never sleeps, right? There will be lots of time to have some fun!"

CHAPTER TWO

The Wildcats were in New York City! After arriving at their hotel, they checked in and regrouped in the lobby. Coach Bolton automatically counted heads as Ms Darbus flipped through her information packet.

"Here are maps of the city," she said, handing them out to everyone. "Here's a Metrocard for each of you, so you can ride on the subway or the bus. Don't forget your umbrella, the forecast says it might rain. Oh, and here's an article that shows a special walking tour of all the greatest theatrical sites in the city, ending, of course, in Times Square! I highly recommend that you follow the route suggested."

Chad glanced at the article and muttered to Troy, "Like I really want to check out a costume exhibit!"

Troy stifled a laugh as Ms Darbus glared at Chad. "I, of course, will be with Sharpay and Ryan all day at the Palace Theater, where the auditions for *Last Bell!* are being held," she said grandly. "It will undoubtedly be the most thrilling experience of all of our lives! But I'm sure the rest of you can find something equally . . . interesting to do."

Coach Bolton hid a smile at her dubious tone. He knew that Ms Darbus couldn't imagine that anything – a world-famous art museum, a visit to Ellis Island or a tour of the Statue of Liberty – would compare to being in a theatre. Any theatre, let alone a *Broadway* theatre.

"All right, guys!" He clapped his hands

together as Ms Darbus headed out of the door with Sharpay and Ryan. "I want everyone to tell me your plans for the day, then I want to check that everyone's phone is working in case we need to get in touch with you, okay?"

"Okay!" everyone answered in chorus. They were practically jumping out of their skins with excitement. After all, who knew what adventures waited for them on the streets of New York?

Sharpay stopped dead in the middle of the street and stared up at the lights that spelled out the words: PALACE THEATER. She was completely oblivious to the screeching brakes, angry honks and loud yells for her to "Get outta the street, already!"

"Look at that," she murmured dreamily to Ryan. "We've finally made it to Broadway!"

"Um, I'm not sure we're going to make it to tomorrow unless you move out of the traffic flow," he said, jumping as a car swerved inches away from his left elbow. "Come on!"

He grabbed her arm and hustled her over to the sidewalk. There, Ms Darbus was reading through the instructions that had been sent to all the musical-theatre hopefuls who were auditioning for *Last Bell!*

"We're supposed to go in by the stage door," she said. "It should be right around the corner . . ."

They followed her to an unmarked grey door and waited as she knocked.

A moment later, a heavy-set man with thinning black hair opened the door. "Yeah?" he barked.

"Hi!" Sharpay gave him a big smile and fluttered her fingers at him. "We're here for the auditions!"

"Yeah, I figured as much," he said, unimpressed. He called over his shoulder. "Hey, Tim! We got two more kids here! See if you can find a place for them." He turned back to them. "Come on in, follow me and don't touch a thing!" They nodded and followed him through the door and down a dingy hallway.

"It sounds like there are a lot of people here to audition," Ryan whispered to Ms Darbus.

"Not to worry, Ryan, not to worry," she said, waving one hand airily. "After all, you and Sharpay are two of the brightest stars to come out of the East High drama department in years!"

"That's so true!" Sharpay agreed, preening a little bit. As the stage manager ushered them through yet another door, she added, "We shouldn't be worried about a little—"

Sharpay and Ryan stopped in shock as they walked into the auditorium.

"—competition," Sharpay finished quietly.

Ryan couldn't breathe. There were hundreds of teenagers, all staring back at them!

"Ahhh." He tried to say something, but his vocal cords didn't seem to be working.

"Breathe," Ms Darbus's voice said in his ear. "Remember, you were the Star Dazzle award winner at the Lava Springs Country Club talent show!"

His eyes widened. "That's right, I was!"

"And you have been studying with *me* for four years," she went on.

He began to smile. "That's right, I have been!"

"And furthermore—"

"Yes, yes, Ryan's very good, but what about *me*?" Sharpay interrupted.

Ms Darbus leaned closer to whisper to her. "And *you* have appeared in 17 theatrical productions at East High, played the lead in the fall play and spring musical, and have been studying acting, tap, ballet, modern dance, singing, stage movement, elocution, stage combat and mime for years."

That did the trick. Sharpay stood up straighter, a little colour came back into her cheeks, and she looked at the rows and rows of other hopefuls with renewed self-confidence.

"You're absolutely right, Ms Darbus," she said. "And all of my hard work has been leading up to this moment! I will not fail!"

"That's the spirit!" Ms Darbus nodded in approval. "Now, let's get a seat . . ."

* * *

A few minutes later, they were settled in the third row. Sharpay was sitting next to a girl of about her own age with long red hair, big blue eyes and an air of complete self-confidence. She gave Sharpay a measuring glance, then granted her a smile.

It was, Sharpay couldn't help but notice, a dazzling smile.

"Hey, there," the girl said in a charming Southern drawl. "How are y'all doing? My name's Anneclaire Littlefield. I'm from South Carolina."

"Sharpay Evans, from Albuquerque. This is my brother, Ryan, and our drama teacher, Ms Darbus." As she made the introductions, Sharpay glanced down at the folder that Anneclaire was holding. On the front, in bold letters, was written: RÉSUMÉ, HEAD SHOT, NEWS CLIPPINGS, AWARDS, ETC. The folder was more than an inch thick.

"I'm *so* pleased to meet you!" Anneclaire

18

followed Sharpay's gaze. She looked back up and gave a little laugh. "I thought the producers might like to read a little bit about what I've done. I mean, I'm sure all these other people–" her gaze swept the auditorium disdainfully, "–are capable of handling the background roles, but the director will need someone with lots of stage experience to take on the lead. Fortunately, I've appeared in twenty productions at my high school, I had the lead role in seven plays, and I won Most Talented Performer three years in a row!"

"Twenty productions? Seven lead roles?" Sharpay's mind reeled. Could it be possible that this girl had a better résumé than she did?

"Yes, indeed!" Anneclaire whipped out several articles and showed them to Sharpay. The headlines read: ANNECLAIRE STEALS THE SHOW!, ANOTHER STANDING OVATION FOR ANNECLAIRE, and ANNECLAIRE – BROADWAY BOUND!

Sharpay gasped. How could she have been so foolish as to leave all of her own press clippings at home? Then she saw the triumphant glint in

Anneclaire's eyes, and her competitive spirit came surging back.

"I see you've done a lot of straight drama," she said smoothly. "Most of *my* experience has been in musical theatre. Of course, that should come in quite handy for *this* audition since we're trying out for roles in a *musical–*"

"Oh, honey, you should read my programme bio," Anneclaire said sweetly. "Three of my lead roles were in musicals. In fact, I choreographed the last one all by myself."

"But, but, but . . ." Ryan stammered. "*I'm* a choreographer!"

Anneclaire smiled at him kindly. "And I'm sure your dances are just real cute, darlin'! Maybe that'll help you win a spot in the chorus?"

His mouth dropped open in shock . . . and confusion. This Anneclaire person reminded him of someone, but who? He narrowed his eyes as he stared at her, racking his brain to figure out where he had met someone like her before . . .

Ryan's thoughts were interrupted by a portly man in a blue suit who bounded out to centre stage and beamed at the audience, rubbing his hands together with glee. He was followed, more slowly, by a tall, thin man with grey hair and bad posture.

"Good afternoon!" he announced. "My name is Herbert P. Smith, the director of *Last Bell!* And this—" he pointed to the other man, who lifted his hand in weary acknowledgment, "—is Albert Lackley, our producer. We'd like to offer a very warm welcome to all of you who have travelled so far to take part in our open auditions! We're very excited about the special promotional performance of our hit musical and the chance to find new, undiscovered talent. Unfortunately, we can only cast some of you in the show, but I hope the audition experience will be rewarding and educational for all of you."

A buzz ran through the auditorium as everyone glanced around the room, wondering who would be good enough to make the cut.

"I'm sure it will be educational for *some* people," Sharpay whispered to Ryan. "After all, press clippings don't win auditions!"

"And your press clippings are probably much better than hers anyway," her brother said loyally. Then a puzzled frown creased his forehead. "Why would she think my dances were 'cute'?"

Mr Smith went on to explain that the audition process would take place in three stages. For the first part, everyone would sing a song of their own choosing. If they were asked back, they would be taught a simple dance routine to perform. And if they were asked back again, they would be given a short scene to read in order to show off their acting ability.

"Easy as pie," Anneclaire murmured.

"Yes," Sharpay said tightly. "I'm *so* looking forward to it! Especially since I won last year's holiday talent show with the song I'm going to sing!"

But when Sharpay's name was called, she walked to the centre of the stage feeling a very unfamiliar sensation – nervousness. She stood for a moment, blinking in the spotlight. That bright circle of light had always seemed so warm and friendly in the past, but now it felt harsh and unforgiving.

"Um, my name is Sharpay Evans," she began. She was shocked to hear herself. Her voice came out in a thin little whisper.

"Speak up, dear!" Mr Smith called out. "You'll have to project a bit more than that in a Broadway theatre!"

He was trying to tell *her* about projecting? Sharpay discovered that a little righteous indignation is good for the nerves. She immediately stood a little straighter, lifted her chin a defiant half-inch and said, clearly and distinctly, "My name is Sharpay Evans, and I'm going to sing 'Love Will Lift Me'." From the corner of her eye, she could see Ryan standing backstage, waiting for his turn. He smiled encouragingly and gave her two thumbs up.

Just then, the music started and Sharpay

launched into the song. Within a few bars, she was lost in the music. Soon she was moving to the rhythm as she sang her heart out. By the end, she was giving a full-on performance that finished with a long, throbbing high C that had everyone in the theatre – even the other contestants – actually applauding.

As she walked off the stage, she smiled smugly at the director and producer. Now *that*, she thought, is projecting – Broadway-style!

Her satisfaction with herself lasted through three more auditions, including Ryan's, which Sharpay judged as very good, although not quite as great as her own. He bounded off the stage, grinning with relief.

"I think I did okay, don't you?" he asked Sharpay.

"Oh, yeah, sure," his sister said absently. She couldn't really pay attention because the person who was auditioning right after Ryan was none other than Anneclaire.

Sharpay's eyes narrowed as she watched the

girl walk slowly into the spotlight and strike a pose as if she belonged there by natural right.

Which, of course, she didn't, because that was Sharpay's territory!

Then Anneclaire signalled to the pianist that she was ready, and she began to sing.

Sharpay felt as if she were going to faint. Anneclaire wasn't just good. She was *great*.

She sang an upbeat pop song that spanned almost three octaves and featured a tricky, syncopated middle section – and, to top it all off, Anneclaire had even choreographed a little dance routine to the song! She ended with a flourish, and the auditorium not only burst into applause, but some cheering as well.

Now Sharpay didn't just feel as if she were going to faint – she *knew* she was! A helpful stagehand saw her turn pale and steered her to a stool backstage.

"Oh," she moaned. "I can't believe it! I just *cannot* believe it!"

"What can't you believe?"

She looked up to see Ms Darbus standing in front of her, her hands on her hips and a dangerous gleam in her eyes. Ryan hovered in the background, looking worried.

"I thought I'd be a shoo-in for the lead!" Sharpay whimpered. "But that . . . that girl! She's . . ." Sharpay hesitated. Even in her distraught state, she couldn't quite bring herself to compliment another performer. ". . . not too bad," she finished.

Tears welled up in her eyes as she added, "It's just like that horrible winter musical, when Gabriella wormed her way into the auditions! It's happening all over again, and it's just *not fair*!"

"Sharpay! Listen to me," Ms Darbus snapped, a steely look in her eyes. "You are not just a very talented performer, you are *my protégé*! All you have to do is draw on the exceptional training that I have provided and you will do just fine! *Do you understand me?*"

Ms Darbus barked out the last four words and

Sharpay, eyes wide, gulped and nodded. "Yes," she whispered. "I understand." She glanced at Ryan, who looked stunned. They had never seen this side of Ms Darbus before.

"Good," Ms Darbus said, nodding with satisfaction. "Now I want you to pull yourself together and start believing in yourself the way I believe in you!"

For the first time since she had heard her new rival sing, Sharpay began to smile. Ms Darbus's delivery may have been more drill sergeant than drama teacher, but her pep talk had worked. She had managed to make Sharpay feel that she could do *anything* – even win the lead role from someone like Anneclaire Littlefield!

CHAPTER THREE

While Sharpay and Ryan were sweating out their auditions, some of the other Wildcats – Troy, Gabriella, Chad, Zeke, Jason and Taylor – had decided to have some fun.

Well, most of them had decided to have fun. They had headed down to Greenwich Village, guidebooks in hand, to check out the area. But Gabriella and Taylor couldn't stop asking each other questions that were likely to come up on the *College Quizmaster* show.

"The father of mathematics is . . . ?" Gabriella asked Taylor.

"Archimedes!"

"Correct!" The girls gave each other a high five.

"And the British author known for his social conscience and moving portrayals of the poor in Victorian England is . . . ?" Taylor asked Gabriella.

"Charles Dickens!"

"Correct!" Taylor exclaimed.

As they gave each other another high five, Chad sighed deeply. "I don't want to spoil the fun here, but we are in New York City," he reminded them. "The Big Apple! One of the most happenin' places in the country, if not the world!"

Taylor gave him a cool look. "And your point would be?"

Chad rolled his eyes in disgust. "Quit studying for a few minutes! Look!" He flung his arm out wide to point to a pizzeria that had clearly been open for many years. Decades, in fact. "Doesn't that look like an awesome place to have lunch?"

Jason lifted his head from the guidebook he'd been studying ever since the senior class trip had been announced. "You're absolutely right, Chad," he said solemnly. "In fact, that restaurant is none other than Pietro's Pizza, established in 1903 and renowned as one of the best pizzerias in the world! The slices are world-famous and–" He leafed through his book quickly, then nodded as he found the right page. "–it's been featured in 13 films, including the classic *Murder by Mozzarella!*"

"Really?" Troy said. "I love that movie! And I'm starving. What do you guys say . . . should we grab a slice?"

Everyone nodded enthusiastically and headed for the pizza parlour. But as they crowded through the door, Taylor murmured to Gabriella, "The Roman numeral MCMXCIX is . . ."

"1999," Gabriella whispered back.

"Correct!" They gave each other a furtive low

five, then looked up at the menu board to choose the slice they wanted to order.

"What do you say, Gabriella?" Troy said in a teasing voice. "Are you going for your favourite combo, pepperoni-and-pineapple?"

"What?" Jason looked up from his guidebook, shocked. "This is New York, man! You've gotta order a traditional slice! Look!" He flipped the book around to show him the section on New York City pizzeria history and stabbed his finger at the entry for Pietro's. "Tomato and cheese, or sausage, or margherita, but *no pineapple!*"

"You're absolutely right, Jason," Gabriella said, trying not to laugh at how earnest he was. "When in New York, you've got to eat like a New Yorker."

They all ended up ordering a simple slice with cheese and tomato sauce. After taking the first bite, Taylor looked at Jason with round eyes. "Your guidebook did not steer you wrong, my friend," she said. "This is awesome pizza!"

Jason nodded, a bit smug. "Wait till we get to

31

the next spot they recommend. The best hot dogs in the world!"

Tension was high in the Palace Theater as Mr Smith took the stage once again, this time holding a piece of paper. "Ladies and gentlemen! We want to thank you from the bottom of our hearts for the effort you put into these auditions. Sadly, not everyone can go on to the next round, but those whom we would like to ask back are . . ."

He began reading off a list of names.

Sharpay had her eyes squeezed shut and her fingers crossed on both hands. "Please, please, *please*," she muttered to herself. "I'll do anything, I'll paint sets, I'll iron costumes, I'll be nice to every understudy I ever have—"

"Anneclaire Littlefield!"

Anneclaire let out a shriek of joy, right in Sharpay's ear. Sharpay closed her eyes even tighter and crossed her toes as well . . .

"Sharpay Evans! Ryan Evans!"

"Yessss!!!" Sharpay's eyes popped open and she jumped up, high-fiving her brother and then Ms Darbus. "I *did* it!"

"Of course you did," Ms Darbus said calmly.

Sharpay sat down again, smiling with happy relief. And silently, she decided that any promises about painting sets, ironing costumes, or being nice to understudies were null and void, since she had muttered them under extreme duress.

Soon the director had finished reading off the callback list. "Please be here tomorrow morning at nine a.m. sharp for your dance audition," he said. "Thank you, and good night."

Sharpay, Ryan and Ms Darbus joined the crowd leaving the auditorium. Half of the people were bubbling with excitement, loudly chattering about what they planned to do to prepare for the next day's audition. The other half were downcast, quietly reassuring each other that they didn't care a bit about not being called back because now they'd have that much more time to go sightseeing . . .

Sharpay grandly ignored everyone. "That wasn't so bad after all!" she said brightly. "I don't know why I got so nervous, it was ridiculous, really—"

"Hey," Anneclaire interrupted. "Y'all did pretty good in the singing audition."

"Thank you," Sharpay said coolly. With all the graciousness she could muster, she added, "Your audition was quite . . . respectable as well."

"Of course, the singing is the easiest part! Tomorrow is where I'm really going to shine!" Anneclaire continued. "My drama teacher says that it's almost impossible for her to decide what my strong point is as a performer, but that she'd have to say that my dancing is even better than my singing!"

Ryan gasped. Now he knew who this girl reminded him of! She sounded exactly like . . . Sharpay!

"I know, it's hard to believe," Anneclaire went

on, mistaking his expression for awe. "Even I was pleased with my singing today, and my biggest flaw is that I am a total perfectionist! For example, I know Mr Smith said that we'd all have to learn a little dance for tomorrow's audition, but I just talked to him and explained that I love *Last Bell!* so much that I've spent the last two months creating an original dance for the big cafeteria number in the second act. And you know what he said? He said he'd be really interested in seeing it!"

Sharpay tried not to whimper. Why hadn't she thought of doing that?

Anneclaire leaned towards them and whispered conspiratorially, "And you know what else? He told me he thinks that the dance they've been using is getting a little tired, so he wants to see if my ideas can freshen it up a bit." She beamed at them. "Now wouldn't that be something? To have a Broadway choreography credit before I even graduate from high school?"

"Yes," Ryan said insincerely. "That would really be . . . something."

"Well, I'd better get back to the hotel and run through my routine a few times. See y'all tomorrow!"

And with a jaunty wave, she was gone.

For a long moment, Sharpay, Ryan and Ms Darbus stood motionless in the lobby. Then Sharpay murmured faintly, "I think I need to freshen up a bit." She headed for the toilets, closely followed by Ms Darbus.

Ryan wandered around the lobby, looking at the photos of the current cast members that hung on the wall. He took a deep breath. Even the air in the lobby seemed filled with the vibrations of legendary performances, thrilling theatrical history and spectacular stories of understudies who became stars . . .

Then he sneezed. It was filled with a lot of dust, too.

After a few minutes, he realized that he had left his umbrella in the auditorium. He opened the door leading into the huge, darkened room and felt a shiver of excitement run through him. It was fantastic to be in the audience watching a show, of course, but it was even better to be in the theatre when no one else was there, he thought.

In the dark and the quiet, you could imagine yourself up there on the stage.

In the dark and the quiet, you could visualize the audience focused totally on you, responding to your performance.

In the dark and the quiet, you could . . .

. . . hear the director and producer of *Last Bell!* talking about the auditions they had just witnessed.

Quickly, he ducked down behind the seats, hoping they hadn't seen him. Not that he was doing anything wrong – he was just looking for an umbrella – but he didn't want them to think he was sneaking around where he wasn't supposed to be.

"Lotta great kids up there," Mr Smith said

to Mr Lackley. "Too bad we can't use them all."

The producer shrugged. "That's showbiz," he said wearily as he double-checked a list. "Is there some reason we had to buy three new costumes last week? And why are we repainting the set again? Didn't we do that six months ago?"

Mr Smith ignored these questions. After all, you couldn't stage a filet-mignon musical on a hot-dog budget. He squinted at the stage. "So I had an idea about changing the production number at the end of Act One," he said. "The cheerleader-and-basketball-player dance is getting kind of tired."

"If you say so," Mr Lackley said, putting on reading glasses and peering at another paper that was covered with numbers. "Why are we 20 grand over budget on lights? Is someone breaking the bulbs every night?"

"Yeah, we need to spice that number up," Mr Smith continued. "In fact, I had an absolute inspiration this morning when I was taking my shower!"

Mr Lackley groaned. The last time the director had an inspiration in the shower it had cost millions.

"I'm thinking we should change the number completely, from top to bottom!" Mr Smith went on. "I'm thinking we should do some kind of historical revue, you know, have the kids doing dances from the past five decades. Flashback numbers are always a big hit."

"I'm thinking it sounds expensive," the producer said gloomily. "I suppose you'd need all-new costumes?"

"A minor detail!" Mr Smith waved a hand dismissively. "This is genius! We start with the '40s, with all the kids jitterbugging around the stage, then move to the '50s, when they're all dressed like Elvis, then the '60s, with lots of hippie clothes and psychedelic lights, and then the '70s–"

"I remember the '70s," Mr Lackley interrupted. After a moment, he added, "I didn't like them."

"People will love it! No matter what age you

are, there will be something for you!" Mr Smith was actually jumping up and down in the aisle, he was so excited. "Let's call Darien and get him to work up a section for the kids to try tomorrow in their auditions. I think the '60s 'Summer of Love' part would be fun, don't you? The kids'll really get into that . . ."

Their voices faded as they left the auditorium. After a moment, Ryan's head popped up and he looked around warily. The coast was clear.

He trotted back up the aisle and into the lobby, where Sharpay, fully recovered, was tapping her foot impatiently.

"Where were you, Ryan?! We've been waiting forever!" she exclaimed.

"Don't worry, it was worth it," he said, smiling slyly at her. "Wait till you hear what I found out about tomorrow's auditions . . ."

He started talking as they left the theatre. It wasn't until ten minutes later, when the rain began to fall, that he realized that he had never found his umbrella.

CHAPTER FOUR

"**W**hoa!" Chad jumped back to the kerb as a cab came hurtling around the corner. "Slow down, dude!"

"This is New York," Taylor said. "I think they're required by law to drive like that." She looked at Chad, who was stunned. "Are you okay?"

Chad took a deep breath. "Oh, yeah. Just taking a little break to make sure my heart is still working. Hey, where is everybody?"

They turned to see Gabriella and Troy staring in the window of a shop that sold only retro lunch boxes from the '60s, and Zeke gazing at the pastries in the bakery next door. Jason was standing right in the middle of the pavement, reading his guidebook and completely ignoring irritated comments from the people who had to walk around him.

Taylor sighed. Greenwich Village was completely awesome, but there was so much interesting stuff to see that it had taken them almost half an hour to walk ten blocks. And they only had a few short days to tour the whole city!

She grabbed Chad and they went back to Troy and Gabriella.

"That *Lost in Space* lunch box is so cute!" Gabriella was saying. "Maybe we should go in and see what else they have."

Jason wandered up. "Hey, look, my book says that there's a park that runs along the river just a few blocks away. Maybe we should check it out, now that it's stopped raining!"

"Sounds good," Troy said.

"But I thought we were heading for the Statue of Liberty," Taylor said. "We can't visit New York and not see that. We're supposed to be checking out historical and cultural spots, remember?"

Chad motioned towards Zeke who was still in front of the bakery window. He looked as if he were lost in a dream – a particularly happy dream, judging by the glazed look in his eyes. "I think it's time to do a doughnut intervention," Chad said. "Zeke looks like he's gone into a trance."

They all laughed and walked over to Zeke.

"Come on, dude, we've got lots of ground to cover," Chad said.

"Look at those cannoli," Zeke said in a dreamy voice. "And the sfogliatelle and the pignoli and the spumenti!"

Chad looked. So did the rest of them. And within seconds, they had the same faraway look in their eyes. Then Zeke pointed to a sign in the window. "Hey, this place has been around since 1873! That means it's historical, right?"

The others nodded.

"And the desserts are all *Italian*, which means they're from *Italy*, which is another *culture*—"

"You don't have to convince us, man," Chad said. "Come on, we gotta check this place out!"

Twenty minutes later, they were on their way again, after having taste-tested a dozen different cookies they had never heard of before, but now couldn't wait to have again. Zeke had spent the entire time talking to the bakery's owner, who had given him several useful tips about cream fillings and then handed him a bag with a few biscotti for the road.

"That was great!" Troy said happily as they strolled on down the street.

"Yeah, but if I lived here, I'd gain five pounds in a week," Gabriella said. "The food is just too good."

"You'd work it off walking around," Chad said.

"And jumping out of the way of cabs," Taylor added dryly.

Just then, Troy caught sight of something that immediately made him feel at home: a basketball court. "Hey, guys, check this out," he said, heading across the street.

The court was really a playground, surrounded on all four sides by a tall chain-link fence. It was about half the size of a normal basketball court. A few people were standing by the fence and checking out the action inside as six guys played a fast and furious game of three-on-three.

The Wildcats joined the spectators to watch. "Man, those guys are good!" Troy said in awe.

"No lie," Chad agreed as one of the players raced down the court and slam-dunked the ball through the bent metal rim.

Jason actually closed his guidebook and put it in his backpack so that he could pay more attention to the game. Zeke nibbled a biscotti as he watched one of the players fake out another one with a sweet move that he vowed to try himself the next time he was on the court.

Soon there was a break in the action. "I'm done. Gotta be at work in an hour," one of the players said.

"I'm outta here, too," another guy said.

As they walked off the court, one of the remaining players said to his friends, "Well, I guess that's it for today–"

"Hey, you guys want a little more competition?" Chad called out.

Troy gave him a startled look. What was Chad *doing*? Sure, the game looked like fun, but those guys were big and strong and *really* good . . .

Two of the players looked at each other and grinned, then came over to the fence. "You boys play ball?"

"You bet!" Jason said confidently. "In fact, last year we won–"

"–a few games here and there," Troy interrupted quickly. He knew Jason didn't mean to brag about winning the championship – he was just proud of what they'd done together – but it might not come off that way to these strangers.

"So," said one of the players, "you want a quick pickup game?"

The other Wildcats looked at Troy to see what he would say. He hesitated. They hadn't come to New York City to play ball, after all, and his dad had reminded them all that the trip was supposed to be educational.

"I don't know," the other player said to his friend. "Maybe we should ask them to get a note from their mommas . . ."

That did it.

"You're on," Troy said. After all, he reasoned, they would probably learn a little something about basketball from these guys, which would make the experience educational, right?

Chad, Zeke and Jason broke into wide grins as they hurried through the gate to start the game.

Thirty minutes later, the Wildcats were wondering what, exactly, they had got themselves into.

The guys they were playing against were named Terence, Reggie, Max and Bongo. Bongo wasn't really tall, but he could hit one three-pointer after another. Terence got unbelievable air when he jumped; he was always taking passes up the middle and jumping what seemed like three feet above everyone's heads to hit his shots. Max was a master at stealing the ball. And Reggie – Reggie was just an immovable object. He'd stand under the basket like a brick wall and the Wildcats couldn't get position on him, no matter how hard they tried. He got every rebound and turned it into a basket. All four of them were extremely fast and excellent at blocking shots, and played the whole game above the rim, slam-dunking the ball over and over.

"Okay," Troy said to the other Wildcats. "Let's focus on the fundamentals. We know we're good at that."

"Yeah!" Chad exclaimed. Despite everything, he still had some swagger left. "Let's show 'em how it's done!"

But when they took the court again, Chad tried setting a pick – and the other team was so fast that another defender moved in and Troy couldn't get an open shot. Max stole the ball and passed it to Bongo, who hit yet another three-pointer. Then Reggie grabbed the inbound pass and made another basket. A few moments later, Chad managed to get his hands on the ball, but Terence stole it and lofted it from somewhere in the stratosphere . . . and that's when the Wildcats started falling apart.

They were so flustered by the kind of game they were in – and the fact that they couldn't seem to counter anything these guys threw at them – that they started taking wild shots, getting more discouraged by the minute.

Finally, Troy managed to twist away from a defender. He jumped and launched a shot. To his surprise, it hit the backboard and dropped in.

Chad gave him a high five and Zeke called out, "Great shot!" But Troy had to face the facts. That was one basket for the Wildcats –

and about 100 for their opponents.

"Not bad," Terence said with a friendly grin.

"Yeah, sometimes luck's as good as talent," Reggie added, not quite as friendly.

"Come on, man, the boys here did their best," Terence said.

Troy could see Chad start to react to that, and he stepped in hastily. "Thanks for the game," he said. "We learned a lot."

"I bet you did," Reggie sniggered. "Come back any time. We hold class here every afternoon."

"Hey, you know we'll be back," Chad said. "And we'll be bringing our A-game, too!"

"You do that," Terence chuckled.

"Yeah, you bring your A-game . . . as soon as you find it," Reggie said. Then, as they walked through the gate, Reggie called after them, "Welcome to the Cage, boys!"

"Well, that was . . . instructional," Troy said. The Wildcats, including Gabriella and Taylor, were walking down the street. The boys were still in shock and trying to work out what had gone wrong.

"I can't believe it! Those guys didn't look much older than us!" Chad fumed. He stopped in mid-stride as a thought struck him. "Do you think maybe they were practising for the NBA draft or something?"

"At a cramped little place like that?" Zeke said. "Not likely."

Gabriella decided it was time to focus on the positive. "I thought you guys looked pretty good, considering you hadn't warmed up, and you weren't used to playing on such a small court, and–"

"And we didn't actually let them steal the ball more than, oh, 30 times," Chad interrupted.

Troy was thinking. "Yeah, we can make all the excuses we want, but the fact is . . . we were schooled."

The other boys looked depressed to hear their captain state the obvious. Then Troy cracked a tiny smile and said, "But that doesn't mean we can't come back, does it?"

"Come back here?" Jason had his guidebook open again. "But I've circled 12 more spots of interest, including the tavern where George Washington gave his farewell speech to the troops . . ."

"And I promise we'll get to at least five of those historic sites," Troy said. Then, with a look of determination, he added, "But I also promise that those guys have not heard the last of us. What do you guys say?"

"I say, yes, we're coming back, and yes, we're going to beat those dudes!" Chad yelled. "What team?"

"Wildcats!" they all yelled in response.

"*What team?*"

"WILDCATS!!!"

Gabriella looked around, hoping no one was staring at them, doing cheers in the middle of the street. Then she remembered. This was New York. No one even noticed.

CHAPTER FIVE

After a little more discussion, the Wildcats realized that everyone wanted to do different things. So they agreed to split up for the rest of the afternoon, then meet that night for dinner. Chad and Zeke headed uptown to check out Central Park. Jason was determined to take a tourist bus around the city and go to the top of the Empire State Building. Taylor wanted to explore a museum devoted to Tibetan art. And Troy and Gabriella . . . well, they just wanted to walk around the city and look at everything. As long as they were together, they knew they'd have fun.

They started to explore Greenwich Village. Unlike the area around their hotel, where the streets were laid out in an easy-to-understand grid, the streets in the Village ran at all kinds of crazy angles. Within five minutes, they were poring over their map; within seven minutes, they realized they were totally lost; and within ten minutes they decided to forget the map and just wander around.

For the next hour, they poked their heads into record shops that sold thousands of old-school records – the kind you had to put on a turn-table. They browsed through comic shops and a secondhand-book shop that had 18 miles of books. They watched jugglers, street musicians and some very serious chess players in Washington Square Park. And finally, they were tired enough to sit down at an outdoor café and have a drink.

"This is so great!" Gabriella exclaimed as she watched the people walking by. "I almost wish Taylor and I hadn't made the *College Quizmaster* finals, so we'd have more time to hang out."

"Yeah," Troy said. "That would be fun."

She glanced over at him. He seemed lost in thought; he wasn't even looking at the street scene. Instead, he was sipping his drink and frowning down at the tablecloth.

"Is something wrong? You seem a little . . . preoccupied," she said.

"What?" He looked up and seemed to re-focus his eyes. "Oh, sorry. I just keep thinking about that pickup game. Maybe if I had better moves, we would have . . . well, not won, but maybe not have embarrassed ourselves."

"Come on, Troy," Gabriella said. "You guys weren't embarrassing. You were just—"

"Outplayed." He tried to smile at her, but he was still glum.

"Hmm." She sat silently for a few minutes, sipping her drink. Then she asked, "So who would you say is the best basketball player of all time?"

"Why?" he asked, puzzled.

"Well, I have a feeling you're going to be thinking about basketball for the rest of the afternoon, even if you try not to," she teased him. "I thought we might as well go with it."

He grinned. "Yeah, you're right," he admitted. "It's going to be hard to shake off that game."

"And I'd rather not think about going on *College Quizmaster* tomorrow," she added. "So tell me about the all-time best player."

"Okay," he said readily. "No question, it was Michael Jordan. He led the Chicago Bulls to six championships in the '90s. He's also a great all-around athlete. You know, he's an excellent golfer." He said that with such a sense of satisfaction that Gabriella had to laugh. Troy was also on the East High golf team when he wasn't playing basketball. "*And* he even quit basketball and played minor-league baseball for a season in 1994."

"Really?" she said. "I didn't know that. So what made him so good at basketball?"

"Well, he could do everything – shoot, steal the ball, rebound, defend . . . and he'd do whatever he had to do to win the game," Troy answered. "But mostly I think he just really loved playing. In fact, he put it in his contract that he could play basketball any time he wanted in the off-season, which most NBA stars can't do. It was called his 'love-of-the-game' clause. Now, let me tell you about the six championships the Bulls won . . ."

"Sharpay! Look!" Ryan had been trailing his increasingly impatient sister through the East Village for what seemed like days. And that was after undergoing the stress and strain of an audition! Just as he thought he might actually faint from exhaustion, he spotted a small shop down a side street that seemed to call to him.

He hurried over and came to a halt in front of the tiny shopfront.

"What is it?" Sharpay snapped. She stopped, looked around, and retraced her steps to find Ryan looking in the front window, his eyes glowing and his mouth hanging half open.

"Look," he whispered, pointing at the window.

She turned to see what had caught Ryan's attention, hoping that he hadn't been sidetracked by yet another aromatherapy shop. Basil-lemon candles were all very well, but they had a mission to complete.

Then she saw the clothes displayed in the shop window. Bell bottoms that flared out over platform shoes. Miniskirts paired with go-go boots and a psychedelic top. Skinny black trousers with ankle boots. Jackets with beading and feathers. Colourful plastic earrings and necklaces. In other words, it was—

"Sixties Heaven," Ryan said in awe.

After a moment, Sharpay realized that he wasn't being poetic. That was actually the name of the shop, painted above the door in rounded letters. "Well, what are we waiting for?" she cried happily. "Our audition-winning costumes await us!"

They pushed through the door into a dim room that smelled like incense. Somewhere in the back of the shop, a bell rang softly, and a long-haired girl wearing granny glasses, patched jeans and a gauze blouse emerged from the back room.

"Hey," she said in a laid-back voice. "How are you guys doing today?"

Ryan got a silly grin on his face. "We're, um, groovy."

She smiled back. "That's cool."

"Your whole store is cool," he replied. "The whole vibe is just really, um—"

"Yes, yes, yes, it's cool and groovy and ever so '6os," Sharpay said impatiently. "But we don't have time for your hippie act. We're in a hurry."

The girl raised her eyebrows, but she nodded and said crisply, "Fine. How can I help you?"

"I need a fantastic 'Summer of Love' costume," Sharpay said, "and I need it *now*."

Half an hour later, Sharpay and Ryan left Sixties Heaven carrying two bags each. Sharpay had put together an outfit (with the help of Angela, the sales assistant) that included hiphugger jeans, a silk blouse covered with orange, pink and red swirls, oversized sunglasses, clunky sandals, and rings for every finger and both thumbs. Ryan had bought faded jeans, a leather vest and hat, and a drapey white shirt that made him feel vaguely like a pirate. He had also developed a serious crush on Angela.

"She said her mother named her Angela because she looked like an angel when she was born," he said with a sigh. "And she still does, don't you think?"

Sharpay stopped in the middle of the pavement and swung around to face him. "Ryan! Pull yourself together! We are going to one of the biggest auditions of our lives tomorrow and we need to be ready. Costumes show what your character looks like—"

"—but acting reveals what your character feels," he finished the sentence with her. They both knew the slogan by heart; Ms Darbus repeated it constantly during rehearsals, especially when cast members complained about the outfits given to them by the costume department.

"Exactly! I need to *prepare*, I need to *feel* what the 'Summer of Love' was like, I need to be able to engage all my *senses* in the spirit of the '60s – and I need to do it *tonight*!" Sharpay clutched her head, the very picture of despair.

"Don't worry, sis, I've got you covered." With a smug smile, Ryan whipped out a flyer that he had picked up at Sixties Heaven. It read: 'One Night Only! Experience Woodstock in Central Park! Performing: The Foggy Prunes'.

Sharpay's eyes widened with delight. "Ryan! This is perfect!"

"I know," he sighed. "Just like Angela."

Sharpay rolled her eyes.

"Hey, that's who gave me the flyer," Ryan said defensively.

That evening, as the sun was setting over the Hudson River, Sharpay and Ryan went to Central Park. They walked along a road that circled a lake, along with dozens of joggers and bikers. When they got to the stage where The Foggy Prunes were performing under a canopy of trees, they saw thousands of other people there. The music started and, before long, everyone was moving and grooving to the sounds of the '60s.

"This is great!" Sharpay exclaimed, watching a man and woman dancing nearby. They were wearing clothes very similar to the ones that she and Ryan had bought, and they had some cool moves that she quickly memorized. After all, there might be a chance to do a few improvised steps tomorrow, and she wanted to be ready. "I'm going to be so much better than that Anneclaire, I just know it!"

"Of course you will," Ryan said absently.

"What's wrong with you?" Sharpay snapped. "You're not listening to a word I'm saying."

"What?" He quickly turned to look at her. His eyes seemed to come back into focus, and he put an interested look on his face. "Of course I am! You were just saying, um . . ." He hesitated. Actually, he hadn't been listening, but it wasn't hard to guess what Sharpay had been talking about. "You were saying that you're going to be great tomorrow! And you will be! Because you're the best singer, dancer, actress and producer on the planet!"

Sharpay eyed him suspiciously – even she thought that was a tad over-the-top – but decided to accept the compliment graciously. "Well, that's true."

"But you know, even if we don't win the auditions–"

Sharpay's mouth dropped open. "Don't even think that!" she hissed.

But Ryan went on stubbornly. "Even if we

don't – which we *absolutely will* – I think it's kind of neat to be here, don't you?" He gestured towards the grassy lawn, the flowers and trees, the band, the music and the people laughing and dancing in the mellow light of the setting sun.

"It would be kind of *neat* to make my Broadway debut, Ryan," she sniffed. "That's what I need to focus on."

But Ryan wasn't listening . . . again! Instead, he was staring past her shoulder, a now-familiar dazed look in his eyes.

"Hey, guys!"

Sharpay turned around to see Angela, still dressed in her hippie outfit, smiling at them. "I'm glad you made it to the concert," she said. "The Foggy Prunes are one of my favourite bands."

"Yeah, mine, too," Ryan said, smiling foolishly. "I mean, I never heard of them before . . . but after tonight . . . well, now they're my favourite band of all time!"

Sharpay rolled her eyes, but Angela smiled

and held out her hand. "That's cool," she said. "Wanna dance?"

Ryan gulped, but managed to nod. He followed her into the crowd, where they began doing some kind of old-school dance. Now that Ryan was in his element, he looked more confident. He relaxed, began smiling and even pulled Angela into an improvised dance movement.

As Sharpay watched, she found herself smiling, too. For a few moments, she forgot the stress and pressure of embarking on a major entertainment career and let herself just listen to the music. And as the band played on, the sun set and the smell of hot dogs and pretzels drifted on the breeze, she had to admit, a concert in Central Park was kind of . . . neat.

CHAPTER SIX

The next morning, Gabriella and Taylor got up early. Way too early, in Taylor's opinion. But they had to get dressed, have breakfast, and get to Rockefeller Centre for the taping of the game show, which started at eight a.m. sharp.

"Are you nervous?" Gabriella asked as they rode over in a cab.

"No, of course not," Taylor said. "We've been studying for months. We are totally ready, girl."

"You're right," Gabriella agreed. "We're, um, bringing our A-game, right?"

Taylor chuckled to hear Gabriella try out sports slang. "You got it."

They got out of the cab and walked to the TV studio. They stopped in front of the building for just a minute to take a photo of the famous golden statue of Prometheus, which overlooked the flags of all the countries in the world. Then they hustled through the lobby and up to the 15th floor, where a production assistant greeted them, took them to a room to wait and scurried off again.

Four other teenagers were already there. Everyone awkwardly introduced themselves. There were two boys dressed in sharp suits. The dark-haired boy said his name was Chase P. Pearson; the blonde boy was Sinclair Farmington.

"We're the Muskrats," Chase said. "From Connecticut."

"You didn't have far to travel then," Gabriella said, trying to make conversation.

Sinclair raised one eyebrow. "Well, you'll certainly score a lot of points on the geography section," he said snidely. Chase sniggered.

Gabriella blushed and turned to the other two contestants. They were from a small town in Ohio where the team name was the Dragons. An intense girl with shoulder-length dark hair and black-framed glasses was named Winnie Barnes; her team-mate, a short girl with red hair, was named Jan Stevens.

"We didn't get here until midnight last night," Jan said anxiously. "Our plane was delayed forever because of bad weather! I just hope we still do okay . . ."

"Oh, I'm sure you will—" Gabriella started to say sympathetically, but she was cut off by Sinclair.

"That's too bad," he said, not even bothering to sound like he meant it. "Lack of sleep can really mess up focus and concentration. But it'll make a great come-from-behind story if you end up winning. More drama for the reality-show segment, you know."

"What are you talking about?" Taylor frowned at him. She'd already decided that she didn't like this Sinclair or his pipsqueak partner. It would feel good to see them go down. "What reality-show segment?"

At that moment, two men burst into the room. One had a TV camera perched on his shoulder; the other carried a clipboard.

"Welcome, *College Quizmaster* contestants!" the man with the clipboard cried. "I'm Bert, the producer, and this is Joe, one of our incredible cameramen. We'll be filming you all the time you're here – as you wait backstage, as you do last-minute cramming, as you have meltdowns in the halls! Every dramatic moment will be captured so that our viewing audience can really *feel* the tension of appearing on a nationally televised game show and being asked impossibly difficult questions!"

Jan and Winnie turned pale.

Sinclair and Chase smirked.

Gabriella felt her stomach lurch.

Taylor just rolled her eyes. Please. As if normal life weren't dramatic enough, she thought. These guys think they have to take it to the next level.

"Now don't feel you have to act or fake anything for the camera," Bert went on. "Just be your normal, lovely selves . . . although, if you feel like you're about to have a panic attack or burst into hysterical sobs, please give Joe the high sign. That's exactly the kind of visual that really pulls the audience in, you know what I mean? Now let's get started with some one-on-one interviews. Who'd like to go first? Chase? Excellent. Let's go next door, shall we?"

When Sharpay and Ryan swept into the Palace Theater the next day wearing their '60s costumes, every head turned to look at them with a mixture of surprise and jealousy. Mr Smith's eyebrows rose almost to his hairline, but then he broke into a grin and came bustling over to them.

EAST HIGH HANGOUT GUIDE

Welcome to East High!
The first day can be a bit intimidating - I know, I've been there. Everyone seems to know exactly where to go and how to get there, but once you've found your way around it's easy. Check out this guide and get to know the coolest hangouts at East High!

Gabriella

DIVE IN

THE HOMEROOM

This is a good place to start. It's where the register is taken (SO DON'T BE LATE!) and it's where everyone in your class meets up at the start of the day. Sometimes we just hang out here in-between class and gossip. Pick a free desk and that'll be your seat for the whole year

THE AUDITORIUM

This is where all of the really momentous moments at East High tend to happen. Principal Matsui makes major announcements about high school events from the podium, like fund-raisers and our amazing trip to New York. It's also where the school dances take place and most importantly where the concerts and musical productions are performed. The auditorium has some really special (and scary) memories for me!

THE GYM

This is spiritual home of the Wildcats, East High's basketball team. In the run-up to a big match the guys can be found most nights after class doing drills. Basketball gets in the way of me seeing Troy, but I know how much it means to him. The atmosphere at the Championship game against West High was totally amazing. Practically the whole school was here cheering on the team (EVEN MS DARBUS!) and when they won, the whole place erupted!

THE CAFETERIA

This is one place you're going to be hanging out – a lot! Hundreds of hot meals are consumed here over the course of the average East High career. It's also where we hang out in-between class, meet up with friends, plan stuff for the weekend and just generally kick back and relax.

THE ROOF GARDEN

This is where Troy and I come to forget about the Wildcats, call-backs and Scholastic Decathlons and just steal a few minutes together. It's so peaceful up here – just don't tell everyone else about it!

THE CHEM LAB

Okay, so unless you are serious into science, then you probably won't be spending as much time here as I do!

THE WASHROOM

Apart from the obvious reasons, you might find yourself in here talking boy stuff or fighting for a space in front of the mirror before those all-important call-backs!

WORK HARD...

Whether it's classes, clubs or sport, everyone at East High works hard and reaches for the stars...most of the time...

THE WILDCATS SPEND HOURS IN THE GYM PRACTISING THEIR DRILLS.

GABRIELLA CAN OFTEN BE FOUND COACHING OTHER STUDENTS AFTER SCHOOL HOURS.

The Scholastic Decathlon team squeeze in an extra cramming session.

FOR SOME, THE SWATTING CONTINUES OVER LUNCH IN THE CAFETERIA.

S PRESIDENT OF THE CHEM CLUB. IT TAKES A OT TO TEAR TAYLOR AWAY FROM THE LAB!

A lot of hard work goes into the winter musical sets.

...PLAY HARD!

Okay, so it isn't all work, work, work! The East High gang really know how to party and celebrate, too!

AFTER A FULL-ON PRACTICE SESSION. THE WILDCATS OFTEN HEAD BACK TO TROY'S HOUSE TO RAID THE FRIDGE!

When the Wildcats won the Championship match it was the coolest thing ever at East High

Even the homeroom occasionally erupts into chaos, much to Ms Darbus' distress!

WHEN THEY'RE NOT AT SCHOOL. TROY AND GABRIELLA LOVE NOTHING BETTER THAN TO LET THEIR HAIR DOWN AT A KARAOKE PARTY!

School's out for summer! The whole school goes wild when the bell finally goes for the end of the school year!

Even though everyone had to spend the summer earning money, they still found time to chill out and have fun!

"Well, this is definitely going above and beyond the call of duty!" he exclaimed. "I didn't ask for it. I didn't expect it. But I'm impressed! Yes, very impressed, indeed!"

Sharpay tossed her head. "It's just a little something we pulled together last night."

Behind them, Ms Darbus beamed.

Then the choreographer clapped his hands and called out, "Okay, everybody onstage! I'm going to show you the routine now. We'll spend a little time practising it, then everyone gets paired up to do it for the auditions."

As the teens filed onto the stage, Sharpay ended up next to Anneclaire. She gave her rival an insincere smile and said, "I love your black leotard. It was so brave of you to go for the minimalist look. And your makeup is so . . . understated."

Anneclaire returned Sharpay's fake smile with one of her own. "Thanks. I believe that a *true* artist should rely on nothing but her talent. As my drama coach always says, sometimes a beautiful jewel looks best in a simple setting."

Ms Darbus scowled as she overheard this. As far as she was concerned, the more elaborate the set and costumes and props, the better.

"I'm sure that approach worked back in your little school," Sharpay said. "But we'll see how it plays on Broadway."

"You bet we will," Anneclaire murmured.

Half an hour later, it was time for Sharpay and Ryan to perform. As usual, Ryan did a very credible job, but Sharpay went all-out: she whirled across the stage, not only performing the dance they'd just been taught, but throwing in some extra moves that she had picked up from the previous night's concert. At the end, the room burst into cheering applause that Sharpay knew was louder and longer than what had greeted Anneclaire after her singing audition.

Beaming with happiness, Sharpay and Ryan ran down the steps to sit in the audience next to Ms Darbus. They watched as other performers took the stage, quietly trading comments about each one.

"Too stiff," Ms Darbus commented.

"Too clumsy," Sharpay ruled.

"Forgot the steps!" Ryan shook his head in disbelief.

"Tripped in the middle!" That stunned all three of them.

Then it was Anneclaire's turn. She was teamed with a lanky boy who had to keep brushing his hair out of his eyes.

"Not a good sign," Ms Darbus whispered. "It's hard to do your best when your partner can't see you."

"Oh, what bad luck for her." Sharpay smiled.

But then the music started and, within five bars, Sharpay's smile disappeared.

Despite her lack of costume and makeup, Anneclaire did not show any lack of talent. In fact, Sharpay had to admit, as she watched in horror, that Anneclaire's simple leotard focused more attention on the precision of her dance steps. And it didn't matter that her partner wasn't that good, because no one watched him for one second. As long as Anneclaire was onstage, every eye was on her and only her.

She finished to even wilder applause and louder cheers. She bounded down the steps and up the aisle. As she passed Sharpay, she said, "Your costume looked real cute up there, honey. And I'm sure the director was only a little bit distracted by all those beads around your neck. . ."

"How long did the 100 Years' War between England and France last?"

Bzzz! Taylor's hand hit the button in front of her. They weren't going to trap her with a trick question! "One hundred and sixteen years," she said confidently. "From 1337 to 1453."

"Correct!" cried the host for *College Quizmaster*, a bouncy man with red hair and a blinding-white smile. "Next question: wind speed is measured by what instrument?"

Winnie hit her buzzer. "An anemometer."

"Correct! Next question—"

"Invented in 1450," she added.

The host nodded, still smiling. "Yes, thank you, but you already got points for the right answer—"

"By Leon Battista Alberti," she continued. "He was an Italian artist and architect—"

The host wasn't smiling any more. "Yes. Thank you. No extra credit is given on *College Quizmaster* for superfluous and unrequested information. Let's all try to keep that in mind," he said tightly. "Moving on, please. Next question: when was the idea of the atom first introduced and by whom?"

Bzzz! Chase's hand hit his button. "Approximately 450 BC, by Leucippus of Miletus."

"Correct!" The host grinned at the audience. "This is the closest match-up I've ever seen on *College Quizmaster*! It's turning into a real nail-biter! Let's see if we can stump our teams with this next question, which has three parts. What was the name of the world's first postage stamp, what was on it and when was it introduced?"

Gabriella hit her buzzer. "It was called the Penny Black, it had a portrait of Queen Victoria on it and it was introduced in 1840," she reeled off.

The host laughed and shook his hand as if it had just been burned. "These teams are on fire today, folks! The Muskrats have 125 points, the Wildcats are right at their heels with 123 points and the Dragons are not far behind with 119 points. Let's take a quick commercial break and come back to see who comes out on top!"

As soon as she was sure they weren't filming, Gabriella leaned over to whisper to Taylor. "Those guys are good," she said, nodding to the other teams. "Really good."

"That's okay," Taylor replied. "As long as we're better." She took a long look at Gabriella. "You're not worried, are you?"

Before Gabriella could answer, Joe swooped in with his camera. Bert was right behind him.

"So," the producer said to Gabriella and Taylor, "you're only two points behind, but you're facing tougher competition than you've ever faced before! How do you feel right now?"

Gabriella gave him a big smile. "Terrific."

"We're right where we want to be," Taylor added, her voice ringing with confidence.

"Those other teams are looking very strong, though. Sure you don't feel a little nervous? Maybe like you're about to cry?" the producer asked, a light of hope in his eyes.

"Not in the slightest," Gabriella said sternly. "This is actually a lot of fun."

As the disappointed producer went to interview Winnie and Jan, Gabriella closed her eyes for a moment and swallowed hard. *Fun* wasn't quite the right word for this experience, she thought. Actually, *terrifying* was a little closer to the mark.

CHAPTER SEVEN

The mood at dinner that night was subdued. Coach Bolton and Ms Darbus took the Wildcats to a famous Italian restaurant, known for serving huge bowls of spaghetti that everyone could share, family style. They expected a lot of excited chatter about auditioning for a Broadway musical, appearing on a television quiz show, and seeing the sights of New York.

Instead, Sharpay was saying, "How could that girl upstage me – *me*! She looked like a waif on the stage! I, on the other hand, looked like a *star*!"

Sharpay and Ryan had both been asked to come back for the acting audition, but so had Anneclaire. Sharpay was still reeling from the injustice of this. "My costume alone deserved more applause!" she cried.

Ryan nodded vigorously, but then spoiled the moment. "And did you hear how people were cheering for her?" Sharpay shot him a venomous look. "They must have had too much coffee," he added quickly.

Meanwhile, Gabriella and Taylor were recapping their day. "I can't believe Chase got that question about nuclear fusion right! I had no idea what the answer was, did you?"

Taylor shook her head. "Nope. And I overheard Chase and Sinclair being interviewed for the behind-the-scenes segment. It turns out they've been tutored for two hours a day for the last year to prepare for this!"

"Really?" For a brief moment, Gabriella felt

sorry for them. "That doesn't sound like much fun."

"No, but it does sound like they're ready for the big time," Taylor said glumly. "Those dudes are so smart, they're scary."

Across the table, Troy and his team-mates were going over their basketball game. "How did those guys spot our screens before we even set them? That's all I want to know," Troy said.

"Dude, I also want to know how they jumped so high, moved so fast and managed to steal the ball every time I got my hands on it," Chad said.

"They don't even play as a team," Zeke agreed. "How did they get to be so good?"

Coach Bolton overheard this. "What are you guys talking about?"

"We got into a pickup game," Troy explained. "And it turns out the competition was a little tougher than we thought it would be."

His dad asked several more questions and, when he found out where they had played, he burst out laughing. "I don't believe it! You guys played in the Cage? That takes some guts."

The boys looked surprised. "Why?" Chad asked.

"It's famous, that's why! Some NBA stars got their start playing the Cage," Coach Bolton explained. "All the best players in the city play there, trying to make their mark. If you even held your own, that's something to be proud of."

Troy and Chad exchanged looks. "Well . . . I'm not sure we even did that," Troy said.

"Yeah, I guess we're not used to that style of play," Chad said.

"Maybe we should have gone somewhere else if we wanted a game in New York," Zeke suggested. "Something more at our level–"

"Whoa, whoa!" Coach Bolton was shaking his head. "You got it all wrong."

"What do you mean?" Jason asked. "We were pulverized."

"Yeah, and that's great!" Their coach laughed at their confused expressions. "The only way to raise your game is to play against people who are better than you are. You shouldn't be upset if you're challenged or even if you lose, because that just means you had an opportunity to learn and improve."

"I hadn't thought about it like that," Troy said, already starting to feel better.

"Yeah, when we play against other high school teams, they probably won't seem as tough after what we went through in the Cage," Zeke said.

By now, everyone at the table was listening. Even Ms Darbus was nodding in agreement.

"That's true," she said. She got a faraway look in her eye. "I well remember the time I was auditioning for the part of Evelyn Halsforth in *Starlight in Sandusky*. The girl I was up against had years more training, but that just made me dig deep into my soul! I discovered inner resources that I never knew I had, and I've been able to tap them ever since. That experience helped me grow as an actor, an artist and a director!"

She sighed, enjoying the memory. Then she remembered where she was and gave Coach

Bolton an approving look. "That was very well put, Mr Bolton – especially considering that your background has been focused on throwing a little ball around a gym."

The coach's expression wavered between surprise and irritation and finally settled on pleased. After all, he didn't get many compliments from Ms Darbus, even backhanded ones!

The next morning, Troy, Chad, Zeke and Jason went to a famous deli for breakfast because Zeke wanted to check out their handmade bagels. Then they stopped by a sporting-goods shop to buy a basketball, found an empty court and spent an hour practising before heading to Chinatown for lunch.

"We seem to be playing better already," Troy commented, after they had all piled into a subway train to head downtown. "I've never seen Chad move so fast, and Jason, those three-pointers you hit were awesome!"

"I keep imagining Terence guarding me,"

Chad confessed. "That gets me moving every time!"

"And I kept thinking about how Bongo would steal the ball from me," Zeke said. "I think if I just do that little sidestep, I can stop him next time. At least, that's what I want to try."

"We only have a couple more days in New York, though," Jason said.

Troy nodded. "I think we should go back to the Cage tomorrow."

There was silence. "Tomorrow?" Chad said. "Really? 'Cause I know I'm moving faster, but I'm not sure I'm moving fast enough. At least, not yet."

"You heard what my dad said," Troy replied. "We gotta test ourselves to get better. If we know that's what we're doing, we won't care if we get stomped, as long as we learn something."

After a moment, Chad nodded. "Okay," he said. "I'm in."

"Me, too," Jason and Zeke said together.

Troy grinned. "Great. Oh, here's our stop. The kung pao chicken is on me!"

When Sharpay arrived at the theatre for the acting audition, she looked around the room. "There aren't too many people left for the last audition," she said.

Ryan's eyes widened. "And more than 200 people started out," he said in a hushed voice.

"Look at it this way," Ms Darbus said. "Now you have even less competition."

"As if anyone here actually offered any kind of competition for me!" Sharpay sniffed.

"Remember, the acting audition will determine who gets cast," Ms Darbus went on. "So I want to see you two get out there and dazzle everyone the way I know you can!"

Ryan nodded earnestly, but Sharpay wasn't listening. She had stayed up late studying the scene they were going to perform today, and she had been doing a lot of thinking. "Do you see Anneclaire anywhere?" she asked.

Ryan obediently scanned the room. "Nope. No supertalented diva on the horizon," he announced. "Oh, except you, of course."

"Hmm." Sharpay smiled to herself. "Well, let me know as soon as you see her, all right?"

Her brother looked at her, half-curious, half-fearful. "Why? What are you going to do?"

"Oh, let's just say that I have a little plan," Sharpay said.

"Ohhh." Ryan nodded in what he hoped was an intelligent way, even though he didn't know what she was talking about. All he knew was that when Sharpay had a plan, everyone else had better get out of the way!

"All right, I'm going to match you kids up for these auditions," the director, Mr Smith, announced. "Girls, you're going to be performing the cafeteria scene. Boys, you're going to do the locker-room scene. Okay! First up, Sharpay Evans and June Lawson—"

"Excuse me? Mr Smith?" Sharpay raised her

hand and ran up to the stage. Ryan and Ms Darbus exchanged confused glances. What was Sharpay up to now?

Sharpay leaned over to whisper in Mr Smith's ear. His eyebrows lifted in surprise, but he shrugged and nodded.

"Okay, people, change in plans," he said. "The first audition will be Sharpay Evans – performing with Anneclaire Littlefield."

Ryan's jaw dropped. He turned to Ms Darbus and saw that her expression mirrored his own.

"Did Sharpay just say she wanted to audition with *Anneclaire*?" he asked.

Ms Darbus nodded slowly, a small smile appearing on her face. "I think so," she said. "This should be interesting . . ."

Sharpay and Anneclaire sat on folding chairs, facing each other on the stage and holding their scripts.

"'Well, the homecoming elections are over,'" Anneclaire read. She gave Sharpay a slight smile and tilted her head just a bit. Even from the back of the auditorium, it was clear from Anneclaire's body language that her character was offering some sort of truce.

"'Yes, and I can't believe that I was elected homecoming queen instead of you!'" Sharpay's delivery was slightly exaggerated, but she quickly caught herself and delivered the next line with more feeling. "'After all, you did work awfully hard for it.'"

Anneclaire sighed. "'Maybe too hard,'" she said, with a slight catch in her throat. "'This whole experience has taught me a lot. About winning and losing . . . and friendship.'" A real tear rolled down her cheek. "'I'm sorry for all the things I did to you, like changing the appointments in your organizer so you missed the entry deadline, and putting food colouring in your shampoo!'"

"'Well, I would have done them to you if I'd thought of it!'" Sharpay added a glint of humour to the line, and heard people in the audience chuckle. Pleased, she went on, putting all the sincerity she could muster into the next line. "'I can't believe it took so long for us to realize that we're actually . . . pretty much alike.'"

She glanced up from the page. Anneclaire was looking right at her, totally in character. She gave Sharpay a little nod.

"'In fact, we're a *lot* alike,'" Sharpay went on, and the note of sudden realization in her voice wasn't all acting.

"'So what do you say?'" Anneclaire read her next line. "'Truce?'"

"'Truce,'" Sharpay said.

Anneclaire smiled at her. "Great. Now let's go have some fun!" she exclaimed.

Sharpay glanced down at her script, confused. That line wasn't in the play . . . Oh! She looked back up at Anneclaire and smiled. "Sounds good."

The director bounced onstage, calling out, "Very good work! Now, let's see who's up next . . ."

CHAPTER EIGHT

"**H**ow's everybody doing? Are we all ready for the final round of *College Quizmaster*?" Bert, the producer, burst into the room, closely followed by Joe, who had his camera on his shoulder. They were already filming, even though it was only – Taylor yawned as she checked her watch – 7:30 a.m.

"You bet we are," she said, trying to sound awake.

"And how do you guys feel, now that it's

down to just two teams?" Bert went on.

Chase and Sinclair gave each other a satisfied smirk. Winnie and Jan had been eliminated in the last round. "We're ready to roll on to victory," Chase said confidently.

"Not that these ladies aren't as bright as they are lovely," Sinclair added, with a nod at Taylor and Gabriella. "But we think we can beat them in the lightning round. We've been practising that for six months."

Bert noticed how Taylor and Gabriella glared at Sinclair, annoyed by his condescending air. The producer rubbed his hands together glee-fully at this sign of friction and decided to egg it on a bit. "Gabriella, you look like you have the eye of the tiger today! Are you ready to *take these guys out?*"

Gabriella opened her mouth to say something scathing, but remembered, just in time, that the camera was rolling. "Um, well, I'll certainly do my best," she said politely.

Bert rolled his eyes. "Taylor, what's your

game plan for beating Team Muskrat? They trounced Team Wildcat yesterday in the literature section. How are you going to come back from that?"

"They can always cross their fingers and hope no one brings up Faulkner," Chase whispered to Sinclair.

Taylor's eyes narrowed at the snide comment. "Since we outscored everyone in the science and maths categories and were tied in the history category, I'm not worried about losing a few points in literature," she said sweetly.

Sinclair shook his head in mock sorrow. "I heard that you guys only decided to try out for *College Quizmaster* a few months ago. Chase and I, on the other hand, have been working towards this moment for two years! For the last six months, we spent two hours every day on drills, we read four newspapers a day to keep up with current events, and we hired a private tutor to simulate the actual game. We're better prepared than any other team in the country!"

"That *is* impressive." Bert turned to Gabriella, who was finding it harder and harder to smile. "What do you have to say to that?"

"Well, the final round always includes more pop culture questions, which I think will give us an advantage," she said evenly. "After all, life is about more than studying, right?"

Chase and Sinclair sniggered at that. "Yeah," Chase said, "you just keep telling yourself that on your trip home . . . *losers*."

"I am so mad, I could just . . . just spit!" Taylor fumed.

She and Gabriella had finally been left alone to prepare for the final round. They had 15 minutes before they were going to be called onstage, and they were both trying their best to calm down. That wasn't easy, since Taylor was seething after Chase and Sinclair's remarks, and Gabriella was beginning to get the butterflies that she always had before going in front of an audience.

"How dare they talk to us like that?" Taylor went on.

"Don't you see, they wanted to make us mad?" Gabriella said. "That way, we won't be focused, we won't be on our game, and we'll lose. Not because they're any smarter than us, but because they got in our heads."

Taylor took a deep breath and released it slowly. "You're right," she said. "I know you're right. And that producer was really stirring it up, too, trying to freak all of us out."

Gabriella nodded. "I'm glad we didn't start talking trash about Chase and Sinclair on camera," she said, "even though they were doing that to us. I mean, come on, a quiz show isn't *that* important."

But Taylor was looking worried. "Those guys *have* spent a lot more time studying for this than we have," she pointed out. "They may be obnoxious when they brag about how smart they are, but they're not wrong."

"No," Gabriella said slowly. "Even when we

were in the Scholastic Decathlon, I felt like we had a decent chance of winning. But these guys are much tougher competition—"

"—and they've been studying for two years, and reading four papers a day, and they actually hired a *private tutor*!" Taylor was starting to hyperventilate. "How crazy is that? They just want the win more; that's all there is to it."

"No." Gabriella's voice was firm. "If they were that confident, they wouldn't have been playing head games with us. And remember what Coach Bolton said? Competing against someone who's good enough to challenge you only makes you better. And Taylor—" She gave her friend a wink. "—we're already pretty good."

Back in the Palace Theater, the level of excitement and anxiety had zoomed sky-high. The finalists had all gathered in the auditorium to hear the audition results. Who would be chosen for their Broadway debut? And who would be forced to watch as a member of the audience?

Everybody crossed their fingers and held their breath as they waited for Mr Smith to announce the cast.

Out of the corner of her eye, Sharpay saw Anneclaire standing in the wings. Sharpay hesitated for a moment, then went over to her.

"Well, the auditions are finally over," she said. "I never thought I would say this to anyone, but I think you're *almost* as talented as I am."

"Funny, I was going to say the same thing to *you*," Anneclaire said. Then she added, "Maybe we're equally talented."

Sharpay thought this over for a second, then nodded. "That dance you choreographed was great," she admitted.

"The costume you pulled together was inspired," Anneclaire offered.

"Maybe we should stick together," Sharpay said. "After all, there aren't very many performers of our calibre out there!"

Anneclaire nodded. "Triple threats," she pointed out. "Acting, dancing and . . ."

". . . singing," Sharpay chimed in. "Of course, I also produce," she added casually.

"Really? I've never done that," Anneclaire said.

"Oh?" Sharpay said, pleased. "Well, it's terribly draining to work with performers who aren't up to *our* standards, but I find it quite rewarding."

"That's exactly how I feel," Anneclaire said, "about all the shows I've directed."

Sharpay bit her lip, annoyed. Was this girl always going to try to one-up her? Then she remembered how her competition with Anneclaire had made her try harder at every stage of the auditions, and how acting with another talented performer had made her job so much easier. She decided that she could, just possibly, learn something here.

"I've always wanted to direct," she said. "I'd love to talk to you about that–"

But at that moment Mr Smith stepped onto the stage, ready to announce his new cast . . .

"This is a three-part question," the game show host said. "What is the largest continent on Earth? What theory states that the continents once formed one large land mass? And what was the name of that supercontinent?"

Gabriella's hand hit the buzzer. "Asia, the Continental Drift Theory and, er . . ." She stopped, her mind blank.

"Pangaea," Taylor said quickly.

"Correct on all counts!" the host cried.

"Thanks," Gabriella whispered to Taylor.

"No problem." Taylor grinned at Chase and Sinclair, who were scowling. "No problem at all."

"Next question," the host said. "Also in three parts. What was the first city to reach a population of one million? When did that milestone occur? And what was the second city to hit that mark?"

Before the last word was out of his mouth, Chase had hit his button. "Ancient Rome, 5 BC and London," he rattled off, adding smugly, "and London didn't reach a million people until 1800."

"Correct on all counts, no extra credit for the unasked-for information," the host said, frowning at Chase. He *really* hated show-offs. "Next question! I will read the opening lines from a series of classic books. Name the title and author of the book. Ready? 'There was no possibility of taking a walk that day–'"

Bzzz! "*Jane Eyre* by Charlotte Brontë," Sinclair said. He smirked at Taylor.

"Correct! 'Call me Ishmael–'"

Bzzz! "*Moby Dick* by Herman Melville," Taylor said. She smirked back.

"Correct! 'Christmas won't be Christmas without any presents–'"

Bzzz! "*Little Women* by Louisa May Alcott," Gabriella answered.

"Correct! 'Marley was dead, to begin with–'"

Bzzz! "*A Christmas Carol* by Charles Dickens," Chase said.

And so it went for question after question. Team Wildcat would pull ahead by a few points, only to be tied by Team Muskrat. Team Muskrat would have a winning streak, only to be overtaken by Team Wildcat. By the last minute of the round, everyone, including the normally debonair host, was sweating.

"I don't think we've ever had a closer contest on *College Quizmaster*," he said. "The score is tied 117 to 117. We have time for one last question. Here it is, the last question of the last round! The winners will each take home a $10,000 scholarship! The losers will receive *College Quizmaster* sweatshirts and caps! Are you ready?"

Chase and Sinclair gave each other smug looks. They looked relaxed and confident.

Gabriella and Taylor just nodded.

"Raising the game," Gabriella whispered to Taylor, who gave her a quick grin.

"Here it is, then, a three-part question: Michael Jordan is considered the best basketball player of all time. For the *College Quizmaster* championship – what team did he play for in the 1990s, how many championships did they win and what other professional sport did he play?"

There was a long silence. Chase and Sinclair exchanged glances again, but this time they looked nervous and worried, rather than smug.

And Gabriella just smiled as she reached for her buzzer . . .

"Hey, look who came back for another trouncing!" Reggie called out.

As Troy, Chad, Zeke and Jason walked into the Cage, they were met by disbelieving smiles from the guys they had played before.

"I thought you boys might wait awhile before taking us on again," Terence said.

"Yeah, like another century," Reggie added. Max and Bongo elbowed each other, laughing.

Troy just smiled. "Hey, you guys have got some great moves," he said. "We just want to check them out again."

Terence looked at his friends and shrugged.

They shrugged back. "Okay, dawg," he said. "You're on."

Troy turned to his teammates. "Remember, let's stay calm and play our game," he said as they walked onto the small court.

"Right," Chad said, a determined gleam in his eye. "We gotta keep our heads in the game."

That was the last chance they had to say anything, because the action was just as fast as before. Bongo kept hitting three-pointers, Terence kept pulling off gravity-defying jump shots, Max kept stealing the ball, and Reggie kept getting rebounds. But there was one difference – the Wildcats were expecting these moves. They didn't get flustered or start trying to make wild shots. When the pace got too fast, Troy signalled his team-mates and they slowed the play down, so their opponents had to match their pace.

After half an hour, they took a break. Sweating, the Wildcats huddled on the side of the court.

"They're still outscoring us two to one," Chad said, breathing hard.

"That's an improvement over last time," Jason pointed out. "That was more like a hundred to one!"

"And this feels better," Zeke added. "At least we're holding our own."

Troy nodded. "And now we can actually see some of their moves in time to react," he said. "Have you noticed that? Now, here's what I think we can work on next–"

By the end of the game, the Wildcats had actually managed to surprise their opponents a couple of times. Chad executed a fast drive to the basket, Troy faked out Reggie and tipped the ball in, and Zeke and Jason thwarted a couple of Terence's jump shots with intense defence.

As they walked off the court, Terence held out his hand to Troy. "Nice game today," he said. "You guys definitely got my respect."

"Thanks." Troy grinned as they shook hands.

"And thanks for the game. We learned a lot from you guys."

"Yeah," Reggie said. "I noticed that. Good thing you guys are heading home, or you'd be making trouble for us one of these days."

The Wildcats laughed.

"Yeah, right," Chad said. "You guys are awesome players. But I know one thing . . . I can't wait to pull some of these moves back home when basketball season starts again!"

CHAPTER NINE

On their last night in New York, all the Wildcats got dressed up in their best clothes and piled into cabs to go to the Palace Theater. They pushed their way through a throng of people in the lobby and found their seats. They chatted, read their programmes, and waited with barely-concealed impatience for the play to begin.

Finally, the lights dimmed, the audience hushed, the curtain rose . . .

. . . and the spotlight hit Sharpay and

105

Anneclaire standing at centre stage. They were surrounded by two dozen other teenagers, including (in the back, at stage left) Ryan. The Wildcats cheered wildly, and Sharpay gave a slight smile in their direction. But then the music started and the first big musical number was underway.

For the next two hours, the cast of *Last Bell!* gave their one-night-only performance everything they had. By the time the curtain came down, the audience was on its feet, and everyone was dancing along to the last song.

The cast came out for their curtain calls, bowing and waving to friends in the audience. Ms Darbus even ran up the aisle to the front of the stage and threw a bouquet of flowers to Sharpay.

"Brava!" she cried. "Brava – and bravo – to all of you!"

Zeke whipped out his camera and took as many shots of Sharpay as he could before the cast finally left the stage for good. "Just think," he said dreamily, "I was here to witness Sharpay's Broadway debut!"

"Yeah, it's a night that will go down in history," Chad said. "Or live in infamy." He paused, then added, "That's a tough one to call."

Backstage, Sharpay and Ryan hugged each other; then they hugged Anneclaire and anyone else within reach. When the rest of the Wildcats made their way to the dressing room, they got hugged as well. In the general excitement, Zeke even managed to get two hugs from Sharpay.

Before they headed off for dinner, Sharpay turned to Anneclaire. "Here's my email address," she said. "Let me know when you're doing your next musical."

"Thanks," Anneclaire said. "I'll send you photos and all my reviews!" Then she caught herself and grinned. "I'd like to read *your* reviews, too, of course."

Sharpay grinned back.

* * *

"I can't believe it's almost time to go home," Gabriella said to Taylor. Everyone was milling around on the pavement outside the theatre and trying to flag down a couple of cabs to take them back to their hotel.

"But we are going home with scholarships in our pockets," Taylor reminded her. She chuckled. "Not to mention the sweet memory of those boys' faces when you answered that last question! Girl, where did that come from?"

Gabriella grinned in Troy's direction. "I had a tutor, too," she teased. "Only he was teaching me all about basketball trivia."

"You're a good student," he teased back. "Being able to remember all that stuff about MJ and pulling it out right at the last buzzer . . . that is awesome!"

"I can't wait to hear about your return to the Cage," Gabriella said to Troy.

"Maybe we can take a walk tonight?" he suggested. "Just the two of us?"

"That sounds like a perfect end to our trip," she agreed.

Just then, two cabs screeched to a halt in front of them. "C'mon, let's go!" Coach Bolton called out.

"Wait a second!" Zeke whipped out his camera again. "Everybody get together in a group . . ."

The Wildcats quickly threw their arms around each other and smiled as Zeke handed the camera to Ms Darbus and ran to join them.

"Say *fromage*!" she called out.

But the Wildcats were already smiling. After all, they had faced their toughest competition ever and they had all come through – New York-style!

Something new is on the way!
Look for the next book in the Disney High
School Musical: Stories from East High series . . .

HEART TO HEART

By Helen Perelman
Based on the Disney Channel Original Movie
High School Musical, written by Peter Barsocchini

The East High auditorium was bustling as all the students filed in for the mandatory Monday morning assembly. When Gabriella Montez walked in, there was so much noise she could hardly hear her friend Taylor McKessie.

"What did you say?" Gabriella asked, leaning in closer to Taylor.

"I said," Taylor repeated, a bit louder this

time, "I can't believe we're missing chem lab for this." She gave her chemistry textbook a big hug. "I love chem lab."

Gabriella smiled. Most kids at East High were happy to have an assembly get-out-of-class-free card, but Taylor was different. As leader of the East High Scholastic Decathlon team, the girl was obsessed with school, especially science.

"Maybe it won't be the whole period," Gabriella said, trying to reassure her friend.

"Students, please come in and take a seat," Principal Matsui's voice boomed through the speakers. Onstage, the Principal was gesturing for students to come in and sit down. He leaned in closer to the microphone that was perched on the podium. "We'd like to get started."

"Hey, Taylor! Hey, Gabriella!" Martha Cox called from the fifth row. Martha was on the Decathlon team and had saved some seats for them. She moved her bag and jacket, and motioned for them to join her.

"Thanks," Taylor said as she sat down.

"Hi," Gabriella said, though she couldn't help but be a bit distracted. Where was her friend Troy Bolton? Maybe he had thought to save her a seat, too? She didn't get to see him before registration, and she was anxious to talk to him. They had talked on the phone the night before, but she always felt like she had so much to tell him.

"Good morning, students," Principal Matsui said.

The audience quietened down as everyone finally slid into their seats.

"It is my pleasure to welcome you to this special assembly about our participation in the United Heart Association Valentine's Day Challenge."

"Valentine's Day *is* a challenge!" someone from the crowd called out.

A roar of laughter came from the back of the auditorium.

Gabriella turned around. She thought it sounded like a comment Chad Danforth would make. Not only was he a great basketball player, but he was also a jokester. In the back rows of the auditorium, she spotted Chad, laughing with his basketball-team buddies. Troy was sitting next to him. Just as she was about to turn back to face the stage, Troy caught her eye. Gabriella blushed and gave a small wave. Troy nodded and flashed her one of his dazzling smiles.

Chad's joke got the room buzzing, and Principal Matsui tried to quieten the crowd once again. He leaned closer to the microphone. "Heart to Heart is an annual fundraiser and an excellent cause. You can all make a difference."

Gabriella turned to look back at Troy again. He was playing with the string from the hood on his sweatshirt. Gabriella smiled. Maybe this year Valentine's Day will be a little different, she thought as she settled back into her seat. As she turned her eyes back to the front of the audi-torium, she wondered if Troy was thinking the same thing.

Principal Matsui was still speaking to the assembly. "This year, Sharpay Evans will be the captain of the event. She will let you know all the details. Please welcome her to the stage."

Sharpay walked up the steps to the stage as if she were at the Academy Awards® in a fancy ballgown. She took her time strutting up to the podium where Principal Matsui was standing. In her red velvet blazer and tailored white wool trousers, she looked like a Valentine's Day art project.

"Hello, East High!" she greeted the crowd, turning on her charm full blast.

Ryan, Sharpay's brother and singing partner, and the drama club co-president, was sitting in the front row. He jumped up and gave a huge *whoop*! He then looked down the row at some of the other drama club members to follow his lead. A few clapped lightly.

"It is a pleasure to be here today," Sharpay said clearly and slowly. She was used to being onstage in front of the whole school. After all, she was the co-president of the drama club and the lead in most shows. Centre stage was her home.

She looked down at the pink note cards that she had carefully prepared the night before. Being the captain of Heart to Heart was a huge responsibility and a big honour.

"Our goal this year is to raise the most money in the county for the United Heart Association. I have devised a plan to help us reach our goal." Sharpay looked up at her audience and gave them another huge smile. "Each school club will create a fundraiser for the week of Valentine's Day. If we all work together, we can beat West High!"

Principal Matsui cleared his throat and stepped forward.

"I mean, we can raise a lot of money for the United Heart Association," Sharpay said. She couldn't help but mention West High. Their rival high school had won the challenge five years in a row. Now that Sharpay was the captain of the event, she was determined that East High would win.

"The drama club will be running the annual

flower delivery to form rooms on Valentine's Day. Forms will be available beginning on Monday." Sharpay paused and looked at her classmates. "Now remember, Wildcats, next Friday is Valentine's Day!"

"And not only that, we've got a game against South High!" Chad bellowed from the back. The students all cheered.

Sharpay smiled and held up her hand for quiet. "With the help of my drama club friends", Sharpay said, "we'd like to present 'Flowers'. It's a little song that we came up with to express our feelings about the event."

On Sharpay's cue, Kelsi Nielsen, East High's most talented pianist and composer, entered from stage right pushing a piano. Ryan leaped up from his seat to join Sharpay on the stage. They had rehearsed this song and dance numerous times. Ryan loved the song. And clearly, he loved any chance to sing and dance.

Kelsi started to play the opening chords while Sharpay and Ryan moved the podium off to the side. They always liked to be in the middle of the stage for their routines.

Ryan got into position next to his sister and gave the audience a smile. Then he tilted his red cap forwards over his eyes.

"How do you say you're special to a friend? What gives you the power?" Sharpay sang.

"A flower!" Ryan sang out in response.

"Yes," Sharpay bellowed in perfect pitch. *"Send a flower and make a donation to the United Heart. You'll be doing your part!"*

Gabriella turned around to look at Troy. He rolled his eyes and put his hands over his ears to block out the goofy song.

The performance had a big finish, with a short tap dance followed by a flip. Ryan and Sharpay held the last pose, waiting for applause. There were a few claps – mostly from the other drama club members sitting in the front row. And, of course, Ms Darbus, the drama teacher, always appreciated a good song-and-dance routine, so she joined in, clapping as loudly as she could.

But there were mostly groans from the rest of the audience.

"Oh, brother," Taylor whispered to Gabriella.

"Oh, brother and sister!" Gabriella said with a giggle.

"They need some new moves," mumbled Martha. She was very into hip-hop and was a great dancer herself.

Principal Matsui returned to the podium and took the microphone in his hands. "Thank you, Sharpay, Ryan and Kelsi, for that interpretive routine," he said. "I hope that all of you will think about how you can contribute to this special school event."

The bell rang, and the students started to head out of the auditorium.

"Please report to your third-period class," the Principal announced. "There will be a sign-up sheet outside the front office. I encourage every club to participate in this challenge. Thank you, East High!"

Taylor grabbed her backpack and stood up.

"Sharpay thinks that this is all about her. Well, this year, the Scholastic Decathlon team is going to raise the most money for the United Heart Association. I'm glad that we have a meeting today after school."

Gabriella raised an eyebrow. The Decathlon team was filled with some great people who knew lots of facts and figures. But what did they know about romance and Valentine's Day?

"Okay, guys," Taylor said, addressing the Decathlon team after school, "we can do this. We just need to think of one great idea."

The team was gathered in a classroom to discuss their fundraiser for Heart to Heart. The buzz in the hallways all day was about the upcoming challenge.

"We're scientific people," Taylor told them. She looked at each one of her team-mates seated at the table. "We can apply logic and brainpower to this problem. We will use proven scientific principles as our guide."

"Love is not scientific," Martha said.

The others nodded in agreement.

"We can come up with a good idea," Taylor said. "It's not like the only way to raise money is by delivering flowers." She got up and walked around the room.

"Well, giving flowers on Valentine's Day is an ancient tradition," offered Timothy Martin, a member of the team. "There's a long history of exchanging agricultural products as part of mating rituals."

"He has a point," Gabriella said. She didn't want to see Taylor upset, but she had to admit that Sharpay had secured the best idea for the Heart to Heart Challenge. They would have to think hard about creating another activity that would raise as much money.

"Maybe we should think outside the box," Martha said. She powered up her laptop. "Let's do some research on the history of Valentine's Day."

Soon the group was reviewing pages of

information Martha printed from the internet. Gabriella stood back and looked at a list of facts about the romantic holiday. But she was distracted, thinking about what this Valentine's Day would mean for *her*. Should she buy Troy a Valentine's Day gift? she wondered. What should she get him?

Taylor walked over to the blackboard. "History isn't helping," she said. She took a piece of chalk in her hand. "Let's try to work this out mathematically. If Z equals love and Y equals Valentine's Day," she said writing the equation on the board, "then all we need to do is solve the equation for X. So clearly the problem is as simple as X equals Z minus Y!"

"The question is, what is X?" Martha said.

"And how much can we charge for it?" Taylor added.

"Is anyone else hungry?" Timothy moaned.

Gabriella smiled at Timothy. Then she said, "My mum always says the best way to a man's heart is through his stomach."

Taylor's face lit up. "That's it!" She rushed over to Gabriella and gave her a huge hug. "Oh, Gabriella," she gushed, "you are brilliant! You are absolutely brilliant!"

Gabriella smiled, but she was wondering what she had said that had got Taylor so enthused.

HighSchoolMusicalDVD.com

HSM
DREAM DESTINIES

In my opinion, everyone has a talent just waiting to be discovered. Just look how Troy Bolton amazed us all with his performance at the winter musical, and how shy little Kelsi has blossomed since we discovered her amazing musical talents. With some pupils the talent is a little harder to find, and with others it shines out – like Sharpay Evans and Taylor McKessie.

Whether it's shooting hoops or being a shooting star, everyone has a dream destiny and mine is helping every pupil at East High reach their maximum potential.

BALL GUYS, DRAMA QUEENS AND BRAINIACS

Where would you fit in at East High?
Which gang would you hang with?
Who would be your best friend?

THE BALL GUYS

The main suspects: TROY BOLTON, CHAD DANFORTH, ZEKE BAYLOR

Never seen without: A BASKETBALL

Usually found: PRACTISING DRILLS IN THE GYM

THE DRAMA QUEENS

The main suspects: SHARPAY, RYAN AND FRIENDS

Never seen without: SOMETHING DRAMATICALLY PINK.

Usually found: PRACTISING THEIR CURTAIN CALL IN THE AUDITORIUM.

THE BRAINIACS

The main suspects: GABRIELLA, TAYLOR AND THE SCHOLASTIC DECATHLON TEAM

Never seen without: A TEXT BOOK OR SOME REVISION NOTES.

Usually found: STUDYING A BUBBLING TEST TUBE IN THE CHEM. LAB.

IF I WAS AT EAST HIGH...

Tick a box
in each row

My best friend would be:

GABRIELLA ☐   SHARPAY ☐   TAYLOR ☐   KELSI ☐

I would have a crush on:

TROY ☐   CHAD ☐   ZEKE ☐   RYAN ☐

I'd be a member of the:

WILDCATS CHEERLEADERS ☐   DRAMA CLUB ☐   CHOIR ☐   SCHOLASTIC DECATHLON TEAM ☐

I would mostly hang out at the:

CAFETERIA ☐   GYM ☐   AUDITORIUM ☐   ROOF GARDEN ☐

My fave staff member would be:

MS DARBUS (DRAMA) ☐   COACH BOLTON (BASKETBALL) ☐   PRINCIPAL MATSUI ☐   MS BARRINGTON (ENGLISH) ☐

My fave event of the year would be the:

THE WINTER MUSICAL ☐   SCHOLASTIC DECATHLON ☐   THE BASKETBALL CHAMPIONSHIP GAME ☐   THE TALENT SHOW ☐

HSM SCHOOL REPORTS

East High School
Report for term ending: 31st July
Name: Gabriella Montez

Teacher's remarks: Having joined the school at the beginning of the year rather lacking in confidence, I have been consistently impressed with Gabriella's determination to do well at East High. She is hardworking and sensible and gains top grades in all the key subjects. She has involved herself in many worthy extra-curricular activities including the Scholastic Decathlon and the winter musical. I am sure that Gabriella has a bright future ahead of her.

Ms Barrington

East High School
Report for term ending: 31st July
Name: Sharpay Evans

Teacher's remarks: Sharpay has a dazzling natural talent for drama and the performing arts. Her voice projection has always been excellent (even when she isn't on the stage) and her role-play goes from strength to strength. She didn't win the lead in this year's winter production, but she took it without malice and bounced back to secure a night on the Broadway stage! A joy to teach!

Ms Darbus

DAY DREAMERS

The East High gang are always wondering what life holds for them. Get inside their heads and find out if their dreams will become reality.

GABRIELLA

"I wonder how long I'll stay at East High..."

"Will I end up being a famous scientist...?"

Gabriella has really settled in at East High, but her biggest worry is that her Mum might make them move on yet again. Wherever Gabriella goes you know that she will always fit in because she is true to herself and she follows her heart and her dreams. She may not be a famous scientist, but she'll definitely be a success.

DREAMS TO REALITY

Check out these top tips to turn your daydreams into reality.

1. Know your talents and your weaknesses.
2. Always be yourself and believe in yourself.
3. Be enthusiastic and throw yourself into everything.
4. Grasp every opportunity that comes your way.
5. Don't be afraid to fail.

GOOD LUCK!

TROY

"I wonder if I'll ever play for the L.A Lakers..."

"Could I really get a sport scholarship to the University of Albuquerque?"

Troy spends a lot of time (possibly too much time) daydreaming about the future. He doesn't know whether his destiny lies in playing basketball, or somewhere else, but when an opportunity comes his way he grabs it and doesn't worry about failing. With his passion and determination, he'll definitely go far in life.

SHARPAY

"I wonder where my career in showbiz will take me..."

"I wonder whether I'll ever be as famous as Madonna..."

Sharpay is so brimming with confidence she won't let anything or anyone come between her and her dreams. She throws herself into everything she does, and even when she takes a knock she soon bounces back! She'll definitely end up on a stage somewhere doing what she loves most, as for being as famous as Madonna – who knows!

FOLLOW YOUR DREAMS

Have you got what it takes to make your dreams come true?
Would you take a chance on something new,
or would you let opportunities pass you by?
Take the quiz and find out!

1. The music teacher happens to hear you singing in the corridor and says she'd like you try out for the choir. Do you:

a) SAY YOU'RE REALLY BUSY ON CHOIR NIGHTS TO GET OUT OF IT.
b) SAY YOU'LL COME ALONG. BUT THEN GET COLD FEET AND DON'T SHOW.
c) GO ALONG AND TRY OUT EVEN THOUGH YOU FEEL REALLY NERVOUS.

2. You audition for the school play because all your friends are, but when you see the cast list you haven't got a part. Do you:

a) YOU RELUCTANTLY DECIDE TO HELP WITH MAKE-UP OR BACKSTAGE.
b) SAY YOU DIDN'T REALLY WANT TO BE IN IT ANYWAY TO COVER UP YOUR DISAPPOINTMENT.
c) DECIDE TO SPEAK TO THE DRAMA TEACHER TO SEE IF YOU CAN GET A WALK-ON PART. YOU JUST WANT TO BE INVOLVED.

3. Your gran knits you a woolly hat for Christmas. It's quite cute in a quirky way, but your friend says it's weird. Do you:

A) WEAR IT – BUT ONLY AROUND THE HOUSE WHERE NO ONE CAN SEE YOU.
B) WEAR IT TO SCHOOL ANYWAY – YOU LIKE IT AND THAT'S WHAT MATTERS.
C) PUT IT IN THE BACK OF YOUR CUPBOARD AND NEVER WEAR IT AGAIN.

4. You get invited to a party by one of the coolest girls in school, but on the night of the party you discover a massive spot on your face. Do you:

a) RING UP AND SAY YOU'VE GOT FLU.

b) SLAP ON LOADS OF COVER-UP BUT SIT IN THE CORNER FEELING SHY ALL NIGHT.

c) TRY AND FORGET ABOUT YOUR SPOT AND HAVE A GOOD TIME – EVERYONE GETS THEM. RIGHT?

5. You get offered a cool job in the summer holidays waitressing, but on your first day you mess up and spill soup all over one of the customers. Do you:

a) GO BACK THE NEXT DAY DETERMINED TO DO BETTER.

b) ASK THE MANAGER IF YOU CAN WORK IN THE KITCHEN INSTEAD – YOU'RE NOT CUT OUT FOR WAITRESSING.

c) PACK IN THE JOB – IT'S NOT WORTH PUTTING YOURSELF THROUGH ALL THAT STRESS!

6. It's the school dance and you are having a great time when you notice that there is just you and your crush left on the dance floor. Do you:

A. GRAB THE OPPORTUNITY TO GET YOUR CRUSH'S ATTENTION.

B. MAKE AN EXCUSE ABOUT NOT LIKING THIS SONG AND RUSH TO THE SIDE.

C. TRY AND GET SOME OF YOUR FRIENDS TO JOIN YOU ON THE DANCE FLOOR.

YOUR SCORES

1. a=0, b=1, c=2   2. a=1, b=0, c=2
3. a=1, b=2, c=0   4. a=0, b=1, c=2
5. a=2, b=1, c=0   6. a=2, b=0, c=1

IF YOU SCORED:

0 – 4 PLAY-IT-SAFER

You turn down new opportunities because you are afraid of being laughed at or getting embarrassed. Try taking on a new challenge even though you are afraid of failing and you might be surprised how much you enjoy it!

5-8 KIND OF DARING

You get quite embarrassed and can be quite shy, but you try not to let it rule your life. You take on new challenges and sometimes it works out and sometimes it doesn't, but you give it a go!

9-12 RISK TAKER

You throw yourself into every challenge and love new experiences. You really live life to the full and are totally true to yourself, no matter what the crowd are doing. Well done!

DOODLE DECODER

Next time you drift off in the middle of a lesson and start doodling on your desk, check out the doodle decoder and see what secrets your scribbles could reveal about you!

DOTTY DOODLE

A drawing made up of lots of tiny dots shows that you are good at concentrating.

SET SAIL

Draw a motorboat and you have an adventurous nature, but a sailboat could mean that you feel lonely.

BOOKWORM

An open book and it shows you are keen to learn. A closed book means you are good at keeping secrets.

FISHY STUFF

Draw a fish and you could be trying to work out a problem. Draw a shoal of fish and you could be a busybody.

CLOUDY SKIES

Small fluffy clouds could mean you need to get away. Draw rain clouds and you could be worrying too much about the future.

EAST HIGH AWARDS

Everyone at East High stands out from the crowd in their own way. Check out the unofficial East High Awards

Most Friendly

goes to...

Gabriella Montez

Having started out as the shy newbie with no friends, Gabriella soon comes out of her shell and makes some awesome mates as well as charming the coolest boy in East High!

Most Determined

goes to...

Troy Bolton

He didn't crumble under peer pressure, or let his own fears hold him back – he went for the Twinkle Towne auditions and proved he wasn't just 'the basketball guy'.

Most amazing outfit

goes to...

Sharpay

No matter what the occasion Sharpay uses her dramatic flair to turn every occasion into a fashion show! Sharpay can't leave the house without matching accessories, handbag and immaculate hair – go girl!

Most Potential

goes to...

Taylor McKessie

Straight-A average, president of the Chem Club, victory in the Scholastic Decathlon – there's no doubt that this girl will go far!

Most Gutsy

goes to...

Kelsi Nielson

The super-talented pianist and composer of Twinkle Towne wasn't confident at first, but by the end of term she is able to stand up to Sharpay – and that takes guts!

THE DREAM DICTIONARY

Ever wondered what your dreams might mean?
Check out the Dream Dictionary to unravel your sleepy thoughts.

Acting
To dream that you are an actor means that your hard work and effort will be well worth it in the end.

Bicycle
If you dream that you are riding a bicycle, it might mean that you need to balance the work and the play in your life.

Crowd
Dream that you are part of a crowd and you need to make some space for yourself. It might also mean you need to stop following others and do your own thing.

Detention
If you dream that you are in detention you could be feeling guilty about something you've done.

Exam
If you dream of an exam, it means that you are being put on the spot to prove your ability, loyalty or truthfulness to someone.

Fireworks
Dreaming of fireworks means that you like to be the centre of attention. It also shows that you are enthusiastic about something in your life.

Grass
A dream about lying in lots of green grass means you are comfortable and happy with who you are.

Hair
Dream of having blonde hair and you will be a true friend to your girlfriends. Red hair means changes are coming your way and a dream of brunette hair symbolizes loyalty.

Island
If you dream of escaping to an island, you can solve a problem by yourself if you take some time alone.

Jewellery
Dreaming of loads of bling signifies inner strength and confidence.

Kiss
To dream of a kiss on the cheek can mean kindness and friendship.

Late
Dream that you are late and it could be that you are afraid of change or seizing an opportunity.

Music
Dreams that are filled with music mean that you need to express your feelings.

Naked
If you dream that you are in public without your clothes you could be afraid that others can see you for who you are.

Outdoor
If your dream takes place outdoors, this symbolizes freedom and tranquillity.

Party
Dreaming about going to a party might mean that you need to get out more and let your hair down.

Quiz
Dream of doing badly in a quiz could mean that your fear of failure is preventing you from trying your hardest at something.

Roses
A dream with red roses symbolizes love, passion and romance are on the cards!

Singing
Singing in your dream could represent happiness, harmony and joy. You are uplifting everyone with your positive attitude and cheerfulness.

Ticket
To see a ticket in your life could mean the start of a new direction, chasing new goals.

Uniform
Dream that you are wearing a uniform and you could feel that you need to break free from the crowd.

Video camera
Dream that you are using a video camera and it could be you need to focus on something without letting anything cloud your judgement.

Warm
Dreaming of feeling warm could mean that you have a crush on someone!

X-ray
Have an X-ray taken in a dream could mean that you are worried that someone might discover you have lied to him or her.

Young
Dreaming that you are much younger could mean you are trying to recapture lost opportunities.

Zip
A zip that does up easily means you will overcome minor troubles.